Army Without Banners

More Handheld Classics

Henry Bartholomew (ed.), *The Living Stone. Stories of Uncanny Sculpture, 1858–1943*
Betty Bendell, *My Life And I. Confessions of an Unliberated Housewife, 1966–1980*
Algernon Blackwood, *The Unknown. Weird Writings, 1900–1937*
Ernest Bramah, *What Might Have Been. The Story of a Social War* (1907)
D K Broster, *From the Abyss. Weird Fiction, 1907–1940*
John Buchan, *The Runagates Club* (1928)
John Buchan, *The Gap in the Curtain* (1932)
Melissa Edmundson (ed.), *Women's Weird. Strange Stories by Women, 1890–1940*
Melissa Edmundson (ed.), *Women's Weird 2. More Strange Stories by Women, 1891–1937*
Zelda Fitzgerald, *Save Me The Waltz* (1932)
Marjorie Grant, *Latchkey Ladies* (1921)
A P Herbert, *The Voluble Topsy, 1928–1947*
Inez Holden, *Blitz Writing. Night Shift & It Was Different At The Time* (1941 & 1943)
Inez Holden, *There's No Story There. Wartime Writing, 1944–1945*
Margaret Kennedy, *Where Stands A Wingèd Sentry* (1941)
Rose Macaulay, *Non-Combatants and Others. Writings Against War, 1916–1945*
Rose Macaulay, *Personal Pleasures. Essays on Enjoying Life* (1935)
Rose Macaulay, *Potterism. A Tragi-Farcical Tract* (1920)
Rose Macaulay, *What Not. A Prophetic Comedy* (1918)
James Machin (ed.) *British Weird. Selected Short Fiction, 1893–1937*
Vonda N McIntyre, *The Exile Waiting* (1975)
Elinor Mordaunt, *The Villa and The Vortex. Supernatural Stories, 1916–1924*
Jane Oliver and Ann Stafford, *Business as Usual* (1933)
John Llewelyn Rhys, *England Is My Village, and The World Owes Me A Living* (1939 & 1941)
John Llewelyn Rhys, *The Flying Shadow* (1936)
Malcolm Saville, *Jane's Country Year* (1946)
Helen de Guerry Simpson, *The Outcast and The Rite. Stories of Landscape and Fear, 1925–1938*
J Slauerhoff, *Adrift in the Middle Kingdom*, translated by David McKay (1934)
Amara Thornton and Katy Soar (eds), *Strange Relics. Stories of Archaeology and the Supernatural, 1895–1954*
Elizabeth von Arnim, *The Caravaners* (1909)
Sylvia Townsend Warner, *Kingdoms of Elfin* (1977)
Sylvia Townsend Warner, *Of Cats and Elfins. Short Tales and Fantasies* (1927–1976)
Sylvia Townsend Warner, *T H White. A Biography* (1967)

Army Without Banners

by Ann Stafford

With an introduction by Jessica Hammett

Handheld Classic 36

This edition published in 2024 by Handheld Press
72 Warminster Road, Bath BA2 6RU, United Kingdom.
www.handheldpress.co.uk

ISBN 978-1-912766-78-9

1 2 3 4 5 6 7 8 9 0

Series design by Nadja Guggi and typeset in Adobe Caslon Pro
and Open Sans.

Printed and bound in Great Britain by Short Run Press, Exeter.

Contents

Note on this edition

The text for this edition was digitally and non-destructively scanned from the first edition. The original illustrations have been lost so had to be scanned from the first edition.

Jessica Hammett is a historian of modern Britain and a public historian at the University of Bristol. She has written extensively on voluntarism, citizenship and civil defence on the Second World War home front, including in her book *Creating the People's War: Civil Defence Communities in Second World War Britain* (2022), and for *Cultural & Social History, Journal of War & Culture Studies* and *English Historical Review.*

Introduction

BY JESSICA HAMMETT

> I was one of a vast army of women, going into action in all the shattered towns, whether they drove through raids, or answered telephones, or worked at First Aid Posts or on canteens, or whether they just stayed at home and endured it. It was almost like being part of a composite personality; their courage was your courage, their danger – yours.

Army Without Banners tells the story of a rural housewife's journey to find her niche on the Second World War home front. After being persuaded by her cousin to join the London ambulance service in the early days of the Blitz, Mrs Mildred Gibson – affectionately nicknamed Gibsy by her ambulance station gang – joins the 'civilian army' of volunteers, an 'army without banners', fighting the 'people's war'. As she goes about her work, she records the fear and boredom of life during wartime, the routines of daily life as civilians adapt to the changing conditions of the Blitz, and the workings of the vast and complex voluntary organisations that supported the civilian population under aerial bombardment. Based on the experiences of the author, the novel is significant for its concern with the role of women volunteers in the war effort. Even if gendered expectations remained entrenched in other areas of their lives, such work took women away from the home and placed them instead on the traditionally masculine zone of the front line under combat conditions.

As one of the most prolific women writers of mid-twentieth century Britain, surprisingly little is known of Anne Isabel Stafford Pedler (1900–1966), pen name Ann Stafford. Her first novel, *Business as Usual*, co-written with long-time friend and collaborator Helen Evans, later Rees, was published in 1933, and her final work was posthumous. In all she penned twenty-five solo authored novels, four with Rees under their pseudonyms 'Jane

Oliver' and 'Ann Stafford', and thirty-six romance novels with Rees as 'Joan Blair'. She also studied art, illustrating some of her novels including this one, and was awarded a PhD in Russian History. During the Second World War she volunteered for the ambulance service in London – an experience which inspired *Army Without Banners* – and she remained involved in social and welfare work after the war, reaching the rank of Divisional Deputy President in the Red Cross.

This novel is part of an explosion of autobiographical writing during the Second World War. There was an awareness amongst civilians that they were living through momentous events and this produced in many 'ordinary people' the urge to record their feelings and experiences for posterity. This outpouring of writing included unpublished diaries, memoirs and letters, as well as novels and short stories, official commemorative publications and local histories. The effort to historicise the war as it was ongoing can be seen in the huge range of official publications and semi-autobiographical literature which began to appear from 1941. Much of this work focused on the Blitz; the period of heaviest bombing between September 1940 and May 1941, when the Home Front became the front line. In *Army Without Banners* we can see this impulse to record the extraordinary experiences of the Blitz. But perhaps of even more significance is the desire to document in rich detail the changes to daily life and, in particular, the new forms of war work being performed by millions of volunteers. With Mildred as our guide, we not only get to know the ambulance service but also tour the vast array of voluntary organisations which supported the population of London during the Blitz.

Mildred arrives in London in October 1940, during a temporary lull in bombing and after her colleagues have experienced their 'baptism of fire' in the early days of the Blitz. The impact of air warfare differed vastly across the country and even within different boroughs of London. During the interwar period government planners had expected a knock-out blow from the air which would result in mass death across Britain immediately on the declaration of war, leading Stanley Baldwin, the former

Conservative prime minister, in 1932 to famously predict that 'The bomber will always get through'. Civil defence was established to respond to aerial bombardment on the Home Front and began recruiting in 1937 into the ambulance service as well as air raid warden, gas decontamination, rescue, first aid, fire and control services. But the 'knock-out blow' did not come to pass, and the early months of the conflict became known as the Phoney War.

The earliest air raids – during the Battle of Britain over the summer of 1940 – targeted ports and airfields and, by the end of the summer, industry. The attacks on civilians intensified with the beginning of the Blitz on 7 September which lasted until 11 May 1941. London was the primary target and over the autumn was bombed for fifty-six out of fifty-seven nights, with 9,500 casualties in these two months alone. But as we see through Mildred, even during this period bombing could feel localised, and on arrival in London she experiences several weeks of calm in her district before her first raid, while the East End continues to be hit. Other large cities such as Liverpool, Birmingham and Hull were also seriously affected, and for smaller cities even a single night of bombing could be devastating as the entire area was impacted by death, injury and destruction of property simultaneously. The raid on Coventry on 14 and 15 November 1940 left 568 dead and 850 injured out of a population of 200,000. Almost a third of Coventry's homes were left uninhabitable, while the Clydebank Blitz on 13–14 March 1941 left around 35,000 homeless out of a population of 50,000.

Although *Army Without Banners* ends with the post-Blitz lull, this did not see a conclusion to bombing on the Home Front. During the Baedeker raids of spring 1942 British cities of cultural significance were bombed and the Little Blitz of January to April 1944 saw the focus returned to London, ports and industrial cities. These were closely followed by the V-weapon attacks (the V-1 pilotless plane and V-2 rocket which were launched from France and the Netherlands) which hit London and the south east between June 1944 and March 1945. In between these periods of intense bombing there were intermittent raids. Although cities were hit hardest, during 'tip and run' raids bombs were dropped randomly on towns and villages along the flight path as enemy planes returned to base, while rural areas of south-east England were badly affected by V-weapons. In total, around sixty thousand civilians were killed by enemy bombs during the war, over forty thousand of them during the Blitz, and almost half in London.

In this atmosphere of intense but intermittent danger, a key theme of the novel is the anxiety felt by civil defence personnel about 'doing their bit'. This anxiety is shared in much wartime life writing. Pre-war recruitment material had told volunteers that theirs would be an important job if war came. But because air raids did not occur as predicted on the outbreak of war, civil defence faced a great deal of hostility from the press and politicians, and sometimes from members of the public in the street. The absence of air raids meant that personnel had no obvious work to do, and the money spent on facilities and equipment, as well as the wages of the minority of full-time staff (about twenty per cent of civil defence personnel), was considered wasteful in the restricted wartime economy. Moreover, male personnel were suspected of joining civil defence to avoid military conscription, and all workers were accused of being overpaid although wages were low and paid only to full-timers. Public hostility towards civil defence is mentioned only briefly in *Army Without Banners*, in Mildred's cousin's letter which summons her to London: 'they used to laugh at us and call the job our war-time rest, chucked tomatoes over the yard fence at us and so on. Now we are busy' (4).

This criticism was largely put to rest with the beginning of aerial bombardment, but it shaped the response to later lulls in bombing amongst volunteers who feared that public hostility might return. This also impacted recruitment into civil defence whose workforce numbers remained under its target strengths for the duration of the war. Recruitment into roles which required particular skills could be especially challenging, and this included driving ambulances at a time when not many people could drive. Indeed, many volunteered in response not to the national recruitment campaign but following personal pressure from friends and family. This mirrors Mildred's experience. She is persuaded to leave her home in the countryside after a letter from her cousin, stationed at an understaffed ambulance station, who writes that 'you could be very useful here. We are short of good drivers' (4). This is enough to make Mildred feel ashamed of her relative safety: 'that sentence about being useful, it hurt; it was like the cruel knock on the door, the relentless hand that hauls you up from sleep when the dream is sweet ... it wasn't enough just to say 'Poor London' when one could be very useful' (4).

Once Mildred arrives in London, we see that the desire awoken in her to be useful, to 'do her bit', and to be an active wartime citizen is shared by the many and varied volunteers whom we meet. But to be fully accepted by those volunteers and enter into their community she must first prove herself. Her colleagues are immediately polite and kind, but 'they had shared some experience together that made a bond closer than any ordinary liking' (26). This is a common theme in representations of military service which, during the Second World War, was borrowed by civilians running the voluntary services under combat conditions. Across wartime life writing many newcomers report feeling this alienation and, from the other side, established personnel admit to being weary of new recruits. Indeed, Mildred switches to this position later in the novel when she grumbles about the inexperience of the new trainees, who 'were paid the same as we were, and we had to teach them' (181). Group storytelling about shared Blitz experiences serves the important function of bolstering workplace relationships – 'those shared nights of flame and ruin had forged a bond between them that was renewed every time they remembered' (35) – while excluding those who joined later. Yet as soon as Mildred has worked under bombardment she becomes fully integrated within the group, symbolised by the switch from addressing her as Mrs Gibson to the familiar Gibsy.

The focus on usefulness and the hierarchies of war work gives us an insight into meanings of good citizenship and drives the narrative forward. The value of work on the home front was often closely linked to its proximity to danger, and this meant that driving an ambulance during an air raid was close to the top of the hierarchy of service for civilians (they were beaten by the men of the fire service). Since during this period most military personnel were stationed in the relative safety of the British countryside, the voluntary work performed by civilians could even be seen as more significant than military service. But – as we already know from the criticism of civil defence during the Phoney War – this status was fragile and dependent on the existence of air raids. Even during temporary lulls in bombing we see Mildred and her colleagues feeling uneasy. After the devastating raids of Christmas 1940, a quiet beginning to 1941 drives members of the team to ask 'if there was any point at all in sticking to the Ambulance Service' (66), and, by March, Mildred complains that 'nothing seemed worthwhile anymore ... All the glory had gone from us – and we missed it' (104). The impulse of Mildred and her friends to look for more useful alternative or supplementary voluntary work reflects the pressure on civilians to be active citizens.

Mildred's tour of the voluntary services of London also serves as an important narrative device as it allows Stafford to historicise the work of volunteers, explore how diverse voluntary organisations worked together to provide support for the civilian population, and tell us why they were important. Many of these organisations were new, established to respond to the unique conditions of aerial bombardment, and even existing organisations had to radically change their methods to face these new challenges. Mildred meets a full range of civil defence and women's voluntary service personnel, post-raid and welfare services, caterers in tea cars and British Restaurants, salvage collectors and a hospital librarian. And on this journey we get a feel for the atmosphere in each workplace, details of the work and the type of people who are performing it.

Throughout these scenes, the role of women in wartime is consistently brought to the fore. Even before Mildred joins the ambulance service she reflects on 'all the jobs I was already doing, the First Aid Post in the village, the knitting groups and the committees and all the local nonsense', not to mention caring (even if at a distance) for her son and husband (6). During the war, propaganda material told women that in order to be active citizens they should take on voluntary work and, by 1943, eighty percent of married women and ninety percent of single women were performing either paid or voluntary work of some kind. Nevertheless, their primary responsibility continued to be caring for their home and family, and the hours required even in voluntary work could be incompatible with the time needed for childcare, housework, and shopping (the latter of which had become far more time-consuming in wartime, with food shortages and rationing).

The work that women were permitted to do was also limited in various ways. Within civil defence for example, women were barred from the rescue service; largely confined to office and control room work in the fire service; they could serve in the ambulance service and at first aid posts, but not in the first aid parties which operated outside during air raids. Even in the warden service where women and men had the same duties, the tasks informally assigned to women by their male colleagues were frequently those associated with their primary role in the war as carers – cleaning, making cups of tea, fitting gas masks, providing emotional support for residents and so on – work that was often neither satisfying to the women involved nor respected by their co-workers. The social research organisation Mass Observation wrote a series of reports that criticised the failure of the government to make full use of the 'womanpower' of Britain, and when Mildred and her cousin Penny visit the Labour Exchange we see the challenges faced by women who want to perform useful work which they also find interesting.

By focusing on a team of women in the ambulance service gender hierarchies are largely avoided in *Army Without Banners*. And despite the difficulties, civil defence could be particularly rewarding for women. In many other sectors of the war economy women were employed to temporarily fill the gaps left by men who had taken on work considered to be more valuable, and they were frequently reminded of this fact. But in some areas of civil defence housewives were told that they had a set of skills which made them especially well-suited to a range of roles, they could do equal work to men, and they could even outrank them. This is explored in the novel at various points. A female warden tells Mildred that 'Probably there were women post wardens, even women district wardens; she didn't see any reason, if it came to that, why there shouldn't be women incident officers. Many women were most capable organisers' (57). Later, we meet a nurse who emphasises her agency at work – 'I like having a job where you can make improvements' (82) – and we are told that in the Auxiliary Fire Service watch rooms are largely staffed by women and 'it is really responsible work; you've got to get the right kind of girl and she's got to be thoroughly trained' (150). Stafford is quietly radical in her insistence on the value of women's work in wartime. By the time we reach the final Blitz scene of the novel, the knowledge we have built up about the various services allows us to understand how the huge and complex web of volunteers are working together, and more fully appreciate the significant role that women are playing within it.

Alongside recording factual details of war work for posterity, the novel gives us an insight into the emotional world of this group of women volunteers. From the first pages we are introduced to the emotional economy of wartime, as Stafford uses the acknowledgements to explain that although 'all the many little acts of self-sacrifice and heroism are true', anonymity was requested because 'This is not only an Army Without Banners but an Army Without Trumpeters'. On the Second World War Home Front every citizen was expected to be useful, and it was preferable to do dangerous work, but it was equally important to be modest and stoical. Mildred's narration is typical of wartime storytelling in focusing on the heroic actions of colleagues rather than oneself and sharing success with the group. After the last big Blitz, civilians repay the service of civil defence personnel through small acts – paying Mildred's bus fare and giving Penny a fresher fish – but the ambulance duty group praise the work of others not themselves. Penny says, 'Some of our people must have been pretty terrific', while Mildred reflects that although 'nothing spectacular had been required of us personally', they may have 'at least been able to make things easier and ... perhaps helped save a life or two' (179).

If *Army Without Banners* explores the anxiety amongst civilians to be 'doing their bit', we are also shown how the Blitz could be a period of deep boredom as well as intense fear. The ambulance station group are irritable and downcast during lulls, and by March 1941 Mildred tell us that they are left 'feeling like old elastic which has been strained so taut that it can't snap back to normal' (103). Meanwhile, methods for coping with fear come up again and again in conversation during the novel, whether keeping busy, being in a favoured environment – driving an ambulance, walking the streets, on a boat on the Thames, inside a building or shelter – or developing rituals and routines to create a sense of normality. Mildred sums up some of the different attitudes adopted to manage fear too, including defiance, fatalism (apparently more popular with men) and pretending to be tough, but she opts for caring more for others than herself: 'this queer, unfamiliar feeling of loving people whether you knew them or not made the blitz bearable' (50).

During the war it was agreed by many that it was easier to cope and control emotions if you were part of a community. The new relationships formed while on duty had a particular intensity – again mirroring narratives of military service – as a fellow volunteer comments to Mildred, 'That's one thing in this job, you make friends, real friends, with all sorts of people you might never have met (128). *Army Without Banners* concludes by looking to the future, and this sense of community is central to the imagined post-war world. War aims, the problem of inequality in Britain and hopes for the future were widely discussed from the first months of the Second World War. Both citizens and their government were urged to think carefully about what the new world should look like, and goals were crystallized in response to evolving discussions of reconstruction and, in particular, the Beveridge Report (*Social Insurance and Allied Services*, November 1942). Civil defence personnel were no exception, but discussions amongst these volunteers tended to focus on the value that their work could have during peacetime as well as war. Many believed that their war work would make them better neighbours and citizens, and hoped that the community spirit they had developed at their posts and stations would continue to make the world a better place.

Thus, as the sun rises on Christmas Day 1941, Mildred muses on the future and speaks for all: 'there are so many of us all in this together, all feeling the same way … We know the things that matter now I think. Kindness and courage and loveliness, and that queer feeling of belonging to each other, minding about each other. I'm pretty sure those are the everlasting things' (184).

Army Without Banners

I October, 1940

The apples were flushed with sunshine; the milky October mists curdled in the valley. Men had died in the air, on the sea, on the beaches of Dunkirk. Women and children had died in Warsaw, Liége, Rotterdam, Dover and many a British town. Much of the battle of Britain had been fought in the air above that valley of ours. Yet we didn't any longer look up fearfully at the sound of an aircraft: the siren still howled now and then like a sick hound, but we didn't go indoors any more, or call the children in from blackberrying.

Only when there was a spectacular aerial dog-fight, low down over the hillside, the air crackling with machine-gun fire, did women straighten up from lifting potatoes, or men check the plough as they drove a neat furrow, or boys lay down the spade as they dug over the kitchen gardens. For the day raids were on the wane, and the enemy was bombing London by night.

When we met in the village, we would speak of London: 'Poor London', we would say, and then we would look away and be silent. We wanted so much to do something to help, and yet, all the time, we were glad in our hearts that our lives were so deeply rooted in the country, that we had homes which must be tended, children who couldn't be left, menfolk on a tough job who really needed us to care for them. But we felt bad about London. We hated the moon when it lay in the sky like a silver feather. We said, 'Poor London', and looked away, not caring to meet each other's eyes.

I, for one, knew that I was glad I couldn't leave the valley. I felt I could bear anything that had to happen, there, in the country, on my own particular hillside, whose familiar heartbeat I could almost hear. So long as I could stay, on guard, to protect the home that George had built for me, where Toddy had changed from a prep school boy to a public school boy and then to an infant lieutenant, I could take what was coming. George was with his ship, Toddy was in the Middle East, but while I stayed in the house they loved, their homing thoughts would always come to me.

Whenever I worried about them, which was pretty well every day, I used to go round the house and make sure that everything was just as it used to be, George's golf clubs and Toddy's books, and his collection of birds' eggs and butterflies. Or I'd go into the garden or up the paddock, and I fancied that if I kept quiet, I could still hear the echo of George's great laugh as he taught Toddy to fire his first gun, the click of his spade in the garden, the chink of Toddy's hammer in the woodshed, the splash of Toddy's feet – such big feet – in the silly little stream he loved to dam.

Some days, it seemed as if I could only believe in the future by keeping the past alive. I felt that if I left, their very thoughts would go astray, so that they couldn't guide the thinkers home. So I just knew I had to stay.

At least, that was how it seemed till Daphne's letter came. It had taken five days to get to me from London, and it had been written in a hurry, on half a sheet of flamboyant blue paper, with a pen that was obviously running dry. And it was just headed: London, Ambulance Station X2, and dated September, 1940:

Dear Mildred,

I've been wondering about you in your nice country cottage; we have had nearly a month of blitz now and it is horrid. Every morning we wake up thanking God we are still alive. You wouldn't know your London, everybody lives in basements or on the ground floor or sleeps in Tubes or shelters.

I'm working at the Ambulance Station just up the road, been there six months. They used to laugh at us and call the job our wartime rest, chucked tomatoes over the yard fence at us and so on. Now we're busy. It's a pity you are stuck down there in the country; you could be very useful here. We're short of good drivers. If you want a war job, here's one that wants you. Only perhaps you'd better not come. Not at your age – and you always were the nervous one. We go out in all raids and at all times. I can't bear bodies and wounds, so feel fearful, but so far have carried through praying loudly all the time.

Enough said. Frightful din of planes overhead. I am waiting to go out – third ambulance. Two have gone already. There's the phone. That means me.

Much love, Daphne.

The first time I read it, I didn't really take it in. I kept saying: 'But this can't be Daphne. Daphne wouldn't be in London. This can't be Daphne, my lovely elegant cousin Daphne, going through all these horrors.'

Because you knew at once that behind the curt words of her letter, there were horrors you'd never dreamed of, horrors you couldn't imagine – and courage to match them. The words of the news bulletins came flicking in and out of my mind … 'Sharp raid on central London … considerable damage … casualties are feared to be heavy …'

But they weren't just casualties any more, statistics on an official form, items in a news bulletin. They were people like Daphne, men and women that Daphne and I had passed in the street, who'd kept little shops where we'd bought cigarettes and cabbages and newspapers, who'd sold us tickets for cinemas and concerts, fitted us with shoes and frocks and hats, coughed over us in buses, sat beside us in theatres and music halls and laughed at the same jokes.

I hated Daphne's letter: that sentence about being useful, it hurt; it was like the cruel knock on the door, the relentless hand that hauls you up from sleep when the dream is sweet.

I could be very useful … 'Poor London …' I could be very useful … it wasn't enough just to say 'Poor London' when one could be very useful. Impossible to pretend any longer that it was enough … if one could be very useful.

There wasn't any longer just one of me, one middle-aged woman sitting in a chintz armchair in a country cottage; there were three of me, one who wanted to rush to the telephone and wire that I was coming at once, the one who only wanted to be left to go on dreaming, and the one who was a kind of umpire at the quarrel. I could hear myself saying: 'But I wouldn't be any use … I'm too old … I'm too fat.' And the other me arguing that Daphne was as middle-aged, if not more so. She had grandchildren.

What she could do, I could do. What she could bear, I could bear. There were thousands of women, feeling just as bad as me, at this very minute, and if they all gave in, there wouldn't be enough people for the jobs there were to do.

Then I heard myself remembering all the jobs I was doing already, the First Aid Post in the village, the knitting groups and the committees and all the local nonsense. And George and Toddy.

All that day, I put off answering Daphne's letter; all that day I umpired, and first the self that wanted to stay would win, and then the self that wanted to go. I tried to escape from both of them by making jam and mothballing George's plus-fours and winding wool and picking fruit. But wherever I went, wherever I looked, I kept seeing London … London streets, the leaves fanning from the trees by the Embankment where George and I had so often walked, and Hampstead Heath, garlanded with fun fairs on Bank Holidays and Toddy straining at my hand towards the swings, the King's Road, Chelsea, on a Saturday night, Mile End on a wet morning, Walworth when the spring sunshine brought the flower barrows out, and Westminster Bridge on a misty day, with the trams grinding across it and tugs wailing from the river. The pictures kept on shifting and changing, blurring into one another, but always as they blended, some woman's figure would usurp the foreground, now sleek and elegant in furs, now shabby in a sagging coat and skirt or muffled in a shaggy shawl with a man's cap aslant above curlers. The face changed with every setting, but the look of appeal in the eyes was always the same.

Whether you liked it or not, all these people were somehow part of yourself; all the men and women you scarcely remembered seeing, the thousands of them you didn't know, their lives impinged on yours, twined round yours, and if you could be useful, then you had to go and help them.

If you could be useful ... but you couldn't be useful if you were afraid. I knew then that I should be frightened, and badly frightened, too. I tried to say that at forty-one, I was past being brave; that I was too old a dog for new tricks.

But at forty-one, you'd had plenty of life, a good long gulp of it, and it had tasted sweet enough. That was why, at forty-one, you ought to be ready to take chances. It wasn't really the young women who ought to be in danger, the young and the gay, who could serve in WAAF or WRNS and ATS, who had boy friends to love them, who would marry and have children, to whom, if they lived, the blessed years of peace would belong. It was the older women who should take the knocks, the faithless generation, nurtured between two wars. People like Daphne, people like me, all the millions of women who hadn't been trained for anything very special, who'd had dull lives, or hard lives or easy lives, brought up their families and seen their men go off to war, the women who wouldn't cut a fine figure in a fancy uniform and didn't care, they were the people who were wanted in the blitzed cities like London.

I didn't wire to Daphne; I wrote. I said I would come up and see if I could be any use and if she could lend me a corner of her basement to sleep in that would be fine.

Before the letter had even left the pillar at the end of the road, I had been to the house agent and arranged to let the cottage, and that evening I began to pack.

In fact, two suitcases were sitting in the hall, filled with the sort of clothes one normally took to London, when Daphne's second letter came. She said I could certainly have a bunk in the basement while I tried out my nerve in London and saw if I could pass the tests for ambulance driving. She added that the house was a bit crowded as a bomb had put a block of flats at the end of the road out of action and some of the people were staying with her; I mustn't expect my usual comforts either, for sometimes the water was off and sometimes the gas, owing to the hole in the road.

So I unpacked the suitcases, took out my best dresses and hats and made a new list. If the gas was off very often, it would certainly be cold; if a block of flats nearby had been hit, Daphne's house might go any night. So the fur coat and the marocain would be better in mothballs. I got out all the very oldest jumpers and tweeds I had and tried to decide which I should most like to lose. There was an old red and blue thing that George had never cared for and that had a depressing lot of wear in it still. It would be quite excellent lor being bombed in. I added George's long woollen pants and a pair of slacks, some fur-lined boots and a leather coat.

Directly the village heard that I had actually let the house and was really off, they came up in ones and twos to offer good advice. They produced letters from nieces or aunts or school-friends who were sticking it out in London, and they mostly read bits – the most alarming bits – aloud to me.

'My dear, Elsie says they haven't had a hot meal for weeks,' said old Mrs F from the house on the hill. 'Not that one need go to London for that, with cook leaving on Monday.'

'Of course,' said the Red Cross ladies, when they came to fetch the spare bandages, 'it's infection that's the real danger … my aunt says conditions in shelters are septic … she has rheumatism already, but epidemics would be worse and you ought to have injections …'

'My cousin writes that all the lights went out in her road,' said another, 'and she couldn't get candles … simply couldn't. I daresay you can't buy a thing, you know. You'll have to live on tins and soda water.'

'Are you going by train or car? Of course, when my niece went by car, she had to spend quite a long time under a hedge, keeping out of the way of a raid. And Mrs Smith's sister-in-law says *they* keep going for the stations; the one she went from was damaged and she couldn't get a train … had to go out to Clapham or somewhere and of course there are no taxis.'

'It's like the Dark Ages, isn't it? Practically living in catacombs with tapers. My husband's sister says they have such a time with *rats* in their cellar.'

'Shrapnel,' said one of the several retired majors who lived round about. 'Shrapnel's the danger.' He began to tell a long story of the eighteenth hole at our nearest golf course by the sea, and how he had just been going to hole out in one when a Jerry flew over so low he had to get into a ditch.

'Had to halve the hole,' he said, 'but the fella was shot down three fields away. Yes, take my advice and look out for shrapnel. Stands to reason, if they put a barrage up, it's got to come down. Take my advice and protect your head; get a tin hat. If you can't get a tin hat, get a saucepan or a colander or anything. Must have protection for the head.'

I quite agreed. I agreed with all of them in turn. I entirely revised my list of necessaries for London and found a large packing case and filled it with my store of tins and porridge oats and dried beans and peas. Even if the gas were often off, you could heat tins on any old stove, even on a bit of fire in a bucket with holes in it. Perhaps we really should come to picnicking among the ruins, crouching round a few coals in an improvised brazier. I packed a haversack full of patent medicines and lots and lots of quinine and bandages: I bought two different kinds of ear-plugs and practised wearing them.

People brought me presents; a neighbour came in with a couple of tins of bully beef; the Red Cross ladies brought an iodine pencil and tannic acid jelly for burns and ointment for mustard gas; the major gave me more good advice and a sack of apples; the farmer's wife brought vegetables, half a hundredweight of potatoes and three dozen eggs. The knitting group came round with a very thick, very broad navy blue sweater they had been knitting for the merchant navy and begged me to accept it. One sleeve might be a hit shorter than the other and they rather thought the neck wasn't right, but it would keep me warm, they said.

By this time, the car was so full you couldn't see out of the back window. It was impossible to think of unloading it at the station and filling the guard's van and nursing the eggs and being decanted at a suburban station from which I couldn't afford a taxi even if it had one. Besides, if one drove up in George's car, one could always drive away in it – if one's nerve was no good, or Daphne's house went.

At the last moment, I remembered what the major had said about shrapnel and ran back into the house for the washing-up bowl and put it on the front seat beside my gas-mask. If I had to drive through air raids, or abandon the car while it was machine-gunned, I meant to protect my head.

I didn't like going; I stood by the car, looking at the garden, luminous with colour where the morning sun struck through the tall grass and the michaelmas daisies, at the patchwork of berries in the hedge, and the first leaves planing down from the elms, and the gentle valley, blurred by mist so that it looked like a child's painting. And suddenly I wondered if I'd ever see it again. The thought stabbed at my breath; till then, I'd never thought that George and Toddy might come back and I might not be there to see them. Now I did, and fear was like a rat gnawing at my guts. I thought: 'I could still get out of this. I needn't go; I can be *ill*.' But I went on walking towards the car, held on the track I'd chosen not by any fine ideals but by a frail thread of self-respect and the trivial difficulties of cancelling a let, re-engaging a maid, sending a wire when the telephone was out of order.

People turned and waved as I drove through the village. One or two called out, 'Good luck; wish I were coming with you.' I wondered if they really did. I couldn't bear to look back at the cottage, but stared at the road till I blinked so that I couldn't see the duck-pond or the thatched houses or any of the landmarks I loved.

As I struck the main road, the local siren screeched. I pulled the washing-up bowl closer to me and remembered the pictures of *What Motorists Should Do in Air Raids*, and wondered just how soon I should put on the washing-up bowl and dive for the ditch. Although we didn't pay any attention to the sirens in our valley, we all had a slight feeling that we ought to respect them more a few miles from home. After all, it stood to reason that the

Germans were bombing something, somewhere; aerodromes, factories, railways and main roads. Specially, of course, main roads to London. We all of us knew people who knew people who really had been machine-gunned.

But though a couple of fighters sizzled across the road at tree-top level, nothing exciting happened. Line after line of heavy lorries snarled along, and the only signs of the Battle of Britain were the banners which flapped across the main street of every village: 'Come and See our Messerschmitt (or our Dornier, or our Junkers 88) and Pay Six Pence for the Spitfire Fund.'

At Staines, something happened. The atmosphere changed just as definitely as it does when you go up a mountain in a funicular. You leave rain-sodden air, in which you huddle into your coat and find it an effort to put one foot in front of the other; you get out at snow level, in sunshine so bright it almost hurts, and there actually is a new quality in the air that quickens all your sluggish body. And coming to Staines, that day in late October, it felt just like that, as if the air were really rarer, as if the courage of all the millions of quiet, ordinary people in that city ahead sent out more urgent vibrations, quickening everyone who came within a certain radius. When I looked towards London, its usual smoky blanket seemed to have lifted, and was crowned with a strange, golden glow – not the cruel reflection of flames; I came to know that well – but the glow of some tremendous spiritual conflagration alight in the hearts of her people.

I drove on; I was glad now that I was going towards London, sorry for the pallid people huddled in the back of cars that passed, laden with luggage, heading for Cornwall or the west. In Chiswick, I saw bomb damage and could not stare because of the traffic. At Shepherd's Bush, the pavements were crowded with shoppers. The police wore steel helmets and respirators at the alert. Horse-drawn coal wagons trundled by, valiant little ponies with vegetable carts and milk carts trotted on, ears pricked.

Once or twice I had to follow a detour to avoid a crater; here and there I saw a road roped off behind a notice saying

Unexploded Bomb. Now and then I glimpsed the jagged outline of a street from which two or three houses had been ripped. Sometimes I saw a whole row of blank-eyed dwellings, chimneys askew, timbers blackened. But always the steady flow of traffic tugged me past before I could feel either horror or surprise.

Daphne's road looked positively prosaic; the burnished trees dripped their leaves into the gutter and an old man was sweeping them into piles and taking them away in a corporation barrow.

When I got out of the car, the washing-up bowl clattered after me; I pushed it hurriedly underneath the seat. Then, as I stood on Daphne's doorstep, with my finger on the bell, London seemed to take a deep breath and let it go on the long steady sigh of the All Clear. I had been driving through an air raid and had never known it.

II October–November, 1940

The girl who opened Daphne's door was a stranger; she wore a green jumper and a pair of men's grey flannel trousers which crinkled over her brogues and pleated round her waist because they were too big. She had soft brown hair that curled by itself, round, honest brown eyes and the sort of smile that very nice children have.

She said, 'Hallo. I'm Belinda. I expect you're Mrs Gibson. Daphne told me to look after you, because she's on duty till eight to-night. I'll give you a hand in with the luggage.'

Together we prised open the door of the car: the washing-up bowl fell out. Belinda picked it up and said: 'How sensible of you to bring useful things.'

I said very quickly that I'd brought a spirit stove and a kettle and an enamel plate and mug as well. Between us we heaved the sack of potatoes and the apples and the crate of tins into the house. And the very old army blanket and the rugs the dogs used to sleep on and Toddy's camping mattress and the haversack with all the quinine in it.

Belinda.

Daphne's hall looked very crowded. It had been an elegant hall, with a beautiful little Sheraton table and a Ming bowl. Daphne had always been very particular about her hall; she wouldn't have letters and cards left on the table or allow you to stand a suitcase on the floor for more than a split second because she said the Ming bowl would be offended if you did. But now the hall was very dark and cluttered up with suitcases, shabby ones, too, girt with string and straps; and heavy coats were draped over the stairs, in preparation for the sort of emergency in which the house was bombed but you weren't and you wanted to arrive at a friend's house with a change of clothes. A bucket of sand stood by the door and an inverted tin hat filled with apples, a leek, a pound of sausages and some knitting wool, lay where the Ming bowl had been.

Belinda saw me looking at it. 'I've just been shopping,' she said. 'You must be wondering why I'm here; but my husband's a sort of nephew of Daphne's and we lost our flat almost the first night of the blitz and she took us in. He's a pilot in the Air Force now.'

I murmured about it's being too awful about the flat, but Belinda said, 'Well, we might have been in it instead of in the pub on the corner. Let's go downstairs and see the kitchen and the dining-room where you can sleep. Mind the step, it's a bit dark. We lost the glass in that window the night the bomb hit Clovelly Court.'

It was quite reassuring to see the kitchen; the window had kept its glass and the white tiles shone and the cat was asleep on the table and the dresser was bright with crockery.

'The bundle under the table is Mrs Dove's bed,' said Belinda. 'You remember Mrs Dove? Daphne's pillar of the house? She's out now, slicing sandwiches at the town hall or somewhere. As if looking after all of us and Daphne weren't enough war-work at her age. Here's the dining-room.'

The dining-room used to look out on the garden; I could remember summer suppers by the open french window and parties which overflowed on to the lawn. Now the windows were covered with wire netting and you looked at a blank wall.

'Blast wall,' said Belinda. 'It's a terribly efficient little shelter.'

Daphne's dining-room had been a period piece – red tapestry curtains, Hepplewhite and elegant prints. Now it was a forest of pit-props, and between the pit-props were half a dozen bunks, gay with check dust-sheets, and from the pit-props hung more coats, civilian-duty respirators, a spare tin hat, pick-axe and saw. There was a medicine chest in a corner, and a galvanised bin marked Water in red. A cheap gate-legged table stood in the middle of the floor, with stools round it.

'However many people are living here?' I asked, looking at the rows of bunks.

'Daphne and me, and Mrs Dove and Barky. I don't really know much about Barky; she turned up after the Clovelly Court bomb and she's mostly out in the East End all the week. Of course, there might be heaps more people any minute. Daphne's given blitz invitations to the whole road. We mostly sleep here, but if you'd prefer to have a room upstairs, you can. There's nothing in it really, but it's quieter down here.'

I said I thought it was nicer to be quiet than solitary.

'D'you want to wash before tea?' Belinda said. 'Don't pull the plug, will you? The water's been off all day.'

After tea, Belinda showed me how the black-out worked and then we walked up the road to the pillar box and came back past the place where Clovelly Court had been.

Even now, the road kept its normal outlines, because the outer walls were still standing in all the hideous irrelevance of Edwardian architecture, complete with pediments and scrolls and useless twirly balconies. But behind them, there was nothing but charred beams, a vertical line of fireplaces with pink and green tiles, and a heap of rubble on which a couple of blackened baths were poised.

We stood and looked at it. We didn't say anything at all.

Overhead, the blue was fading out of the sky and the barrage balloons, like flying pigs, blushed in the sunset. There was a crack and a plop. Another crack, a series of staccato barks.

'Guns,' said Belinda. 'The siren'll go in ten minutes.'

I wanted to run very quickly down the road; but Belinda sauntered, talking about guns. It seemed that there were all sorts of guns and they sounded different, according to the angle and direction of fire. 'Those are miles away,' she said. 'There's no need to take any notice of them. You'll hear the Park guns soon … that's more like it. I expect that's one of the guns on the Heath.'

The siren went. Belinda went on talking about guns. She stopped and turned towards the Park, so that at the next bark I should appreciate her point.

Overhead there was the uneasy drone of aircraft.

Back in the house, we waited dinner for Daphne.

Mrs Dove came in, with a shopping basket full of cereals and fruit and canned soup. Apparently one could still buy quite a lot of things in London. She said: 'Well now, I'm glad to see you, Mrs Gibson. And how're you keeping? It'll be company for Mrs Pennant, having you to walk up to that nasty Station in the barradge.'

Mrs Dove.

I asked after Mrs Dove's family and her rheumatics and the bad leg that was so troublesome.

'To tell you the truth,' she said, 'I haven't had time to feel it. There's a lot of things you're too busy to notice now, and just as well. I made up your bed in the spare room. You don't want to go sleeping in that nasty shelter. Mark my words, upstairs is best – if there's trouble, you come down with the debreeze.'

She departed to begin cooking supper on a glimmer of gas. The crackle of the nearer guns made the china figures on Daphne's mantelpiece clatter; every now and then the house shook itself, like a dog coming out of cold water. I began to fidget with the evening paper, realising that I'd read the front page three times without knowing what was on. it.

'There's nothing coming *down*, you know,' said Belinda, picking up her knitting.

At five past eight, there was a bang on the door. Belinda got up and put out the hall light and opened the door and Daphne came in. Her tin hat was over one ear; she had a brilliant scarf

Daphne, or Penny.

round her throat and her uniform coat, cotton and skimpy on the shoulders, was braced round her till it too had a musical comedy air. Somehow, she carried courage with her like a torch.

'Sherry,' she said, flinging her arms around my neck and waving a bottle at the same time. 'Got it at lunch time to drink your health. It's simply marvellous, seeing you again. Has Belinda looked after you nicely?'

'She's been teaching me about gunfire,' I said.

'That very sharp crack,' said Belinda importantly. 'There – that one – the middle note – that's our gun.'

'Very quiet to-night,' said Daphne, hanging her tin hat on the door-knob. 'Some nights, I fairly run home. But to-night I only ran to see you, darling.'

Belinda agreed that it was very quiet and Daphne said, 'So disappointing. I mean, you ought to be in a really good raid, Mildred. Otherwise, you can't know what it's like. Really, you mustn't go by this.'

The house shook.

'Oh,' I said, 'this is scarcely a raid then?'

'Nothing at all,' said Daphne.

'Feeble,' said Belinda.

Daphne began to pour out the sherry. Then she looked up. There was a high-pitched squeal that grew to a shriek. Daphne put down the decanter, and she and Belinda came towards the sofa, their chins cocked towards the ceiling, their knees bent, rather as if they were doing the Lambeth Walk. A second scream and a third ended in a distant thud – and Daphne and Belinda straightened their knees.

Daphne said, 'Er – have some sherry. It's drinkable.'

I closed my mouth, aware that it had been hanging open for some time. Just for a moment I wondered if Daphne and Belinda had possibly been going to take cover behind the sofa and if this was the right thing to do. But I didn't like to ask and just then the bell went for supper.

There was soup and stuffed marrow and chocolate pudding and black coffee. Evidently air raids didn't much affect Mrs Dove's gift for cooking. We talked about Daphne's grandchildren and George and Toddy and friends and relations and the picnics we used to have as children and it wasn't till we were tucked up in the shelter bunks, in defiance of Mrs Dove and her theories about debris, that Daphne mentioned the Ambulance Station.

'I don't suppose,' she said, frowning a little, 'that they'll be called out to-night. Those bombs were boroughs away, wouldn't you think, Belinda?'

'Anyway,' she added, as Belinda only grunted, 'I've arranged all about you, Mildred. You're definitely joining the Service, of course. But you can't do a thing till you've taken your test.'

'I expect I won't pass it,' I said anxiously.

'You've got to. We're short of drivers. I've arranged it all. You're to go up to Central tomorrow at ten for the test, and there's a letter in my pocket from our Station Officer about it.'

'I-I d-d-don't think I could drive in all this noise,' I said.

'Now don't be tiresome,' said Daphne skittishly. 'All you've got to do to pass the test is to double de-clutch every time you change gear. They love that. I've told everybody what a good driver you are; in fact you've practically passed already.'

Belinda got up very early next day because she drove mobile canteens and they started their rounds at nine, and Daphne saw me out of the house punctually at ten. The siren went. 'You know you don't take any notice of day raids now, don't you?' said Daphne firmly. 'Here's the letter about you … and mind you double de-clutch.'

There was a really nasty ruin at the corner of the road by Central; it looked as if the tops of the houses had been sliced off by a breadknife and the crumbs tossed carelessly into the adjoining gardens. The street was still a tangle of hose-pipes and a couple of demolition men were working on one mound, filling baskets with fragments. A lorry loaded with tackle stood alongside. The house opposite hadn't even had its windows cracked, and a lady with a fringe, in a pink wrapper, was sitting at her bay window staring and sipping tea.

Just as I was wondering if Central really were still standing, a white ambulance whined out of an inconspicuous entrance, and while I was making up my mind to go in, a little man in blue overalls, with a line of frayed medal ribbons, and a tin hat on the back of his head popped out and said:

'Your pass, please miss?'

Instantly, I felt extremely guilty and convinced that I had left the letter at home and should never get to the driving test at all and automatically be returned as unsuitable. I hunted through all my pockets, pulling out old bills and a letter from Toddy and a laundry list, until at last I found the thing lodged in my left glove where I used to keep sixpences for Sunday church.

'First door on the right past the sandbags.'

I went in. Ahead was a big covered yard, ringed with ambulances of varying degrees of whiteness. A telephone rang in an adjoining office and two men in the navy blue, piped orange, uniform of the regular ambulance service, strolled across and climbed deliberately into the nearest ambulance, and a disc marked Accident popped out of the roof and they moved off sedately. To the right was a hideous utilitarian red brick building, windows hidden by sandbags, doors masked by sandbags. A cat was asleep on one pile and a belated, obstinate chrysanthemum struggled at the foot of another. Spikes of grass pricked through the sacking, so that the rounded bags looked like the bald scalps of old men who had dyed their last hairs green.

I edged past them into a passage dark and pit-propped as a coal-mine and fumbled to the door on the right.

Inside, three young women with tin hats on the backs of their heads were filing and card-indexing and writing. Another sat by the sandbagged window with her feet up, reading *Vogue.*

They were all smiles and kindness. Indeed, they knew all about me; there had been telephone messages and letters. I was expected for a test – just a few formalities, a form or two, to fill in first. What was my age and sex? The name and profession of my father … my mother's maiden name, my maiden name, my husband's profession, his nationality, my nationality, my experience with First Aid, with Gas, and the state of my licence?

'It's *clean*, isn't it?' smiled the girl at the desk.

Certainly it was clean, clean these ten years. And had I ever driven a van, a lorry, a private car? And could I do running repairs?

I murmured that I could just change a tyre but preferred not to. They said that did not count. But it didn't really matter and I could go out for my test.

The girl in the window looked up from *Vogue.*

'The siren's on,' she said.

'Too bad. You'll have to wait. It's been on an hour already. You're sure it's still on, dear?'

The girl in the window was sure. She said she had found a perfectly cute jumper pattern, only she didn't know if the neck would suit her. They stopped typing and filing and card-indexing and considered it.

I sat down on a hard chair by the door. Presently a plump woman in a red turban swung cheerfully in. She wore a red reefer jacket and blue trousers with a white pin stripe and high-heeled navy shoes piped with white.

'Morning all,' she said. 'Going to let me through to-day?'

'So sorry – the siren's on.'

'Aw,' she begged, 'ferget it.'

But they would not, even though she pleaded with them for the sake of the shop she had left with no one but her old Dad to mind it. '*Customers* don't stop at 'ome for a sirene,' she said scornfully.

I wondered why on earth people who were going to drive through all raids at all hours of the day and night shouldn't begin by having lessons in a not very noisy alert. Afterwards I decided that it was something to do with insurance.

At last someone said wasn't that the All Clear, and the girl in the window yawned and put down *Vogue* and took off her tin hat and tied a pale blue scarf round her head and slung her gas mask on her shoulder and marched me out across the yard to one of the not-so-white ambulances that stood in a corner.

It felt like a very old-fashioned bus; the steering wheel hit you in the chest, and if you sat on a cushion, you slipped off every time you pushed the clutch; the handbrake made your fingers ache as you pressed the catch, and the whole monstrous vehicle seemed too broad for any gate and too long to corner.

The engine wheezed reluctantly and coughed a protest as I edged in the gear.

'Double de-clutch changing up as well as changing down and you'll find it quite easy,' said the girl who had suddenly changed from a pretty little creature flipping over dress patterns to a ferocious and formidable instructor.

In twenty minutes the sweat was running into my eyes: my hands were shaking: my left leg had paralysis and my right had pins and needles. I had stalled the engine four times, taken the kerb at one corner and practically scraped a bus at the next: the more I thought about double-de-clutching the less I could do it, and I could see no means of getting the ambulance back unless I drove in bottom gear all the way.

By the time I got back, I was wondering how on earth I should ever face Daphne and whether I should ever dare to drive any car ever again.

'You only want a little practice,' said the instructor. 'Come again tomorrow.'

'You should have been back before,' said the girl in the office when we went in to fill in another form or two. 'There's a siren on. Didn't you hear it?'

'I was changing down at the time,' I said.

III November, 1940

All that week I seemed to be either waiting to drive white ambulances or driving them – specially in bed at night. Sleeping uneasily to the crackle of gunfire, I would wake with one wheel of the ambulance in a crater and the other in somebody's first floor window. My left leg had permanent cramp from the clutch.

Every evening, Daphne said, 'Haven't you passed your test yet? Oh dear; I told them you were such a good driver.'

And every day I drove about London. Sometimes we went down streets in which almost every house was shattered, past the tattered remains of buildings where Pioneers were balancing on girders, knocking down unsafe walls and heaving lumps of masonry about. Other times we drove down streets so clean and bright that you couldn't believe they'd ever heard a siren. But always, everywhere, there was a surge of traffic; delivery vans, coal carts, buses and coster carts, army lorries, mobile canteens, doctors' cars, official cars and ordinary cars, throbbing and pulsing down arteries narrowed here and there by craters.

Old men still sold fruit and flowers in the streets; women still scanned the barrows for bargains or peered into the tiny panes let into the plywood shutters of once spacious shop windows. Union Jacks fluttered over heaps of rubble; ribald placards made a jest of disaster.

But outside every Tube station, there were rows of patient women and children, old men and lanky boys, waiting, waiting in the autumn sunshine, waiting in drizzling rain, waiting in the first frosts, waiting in smudgy fogs, just simply waiting for dusk when they could go underground again. They were the city's cave dwellers, whose homes, perhaps, were dust beneath a Union Jack, whose nerve was shaken, who only saw the daylight while they queued up for another night's shelter. People whose nerves were shaken, yes; people who were obsessed by a nightmare need for keeping safe, but all the same, they were people who were sticking by their city, indifferent to the

Up from the shelter.

pleadings and bullyings of official appeals for evacuation. They wouldn't leave while there was a shelter left.

Those were days when lorries brought cans of water to householders in districts where the mains had gone, when Oxford Street and Piccadilly stank of charred timber and wet rubble, when you coughed and sneezed your way through a haze of brick dust and walked in the middle of the road because people hurled dustpans full of broken glass out of their windows on to the pavement, much as two hundred years before, women had thrown slops into the gutter. And when I went to call on my grave and stately solicitor, I found him sitting wrapped in a travelling rug, his feet in a foot muff, in a windowless room, while his clerk swept up the glass round him.

At last one day when I had stalled my ambulance shamingly in a line of traffic at Notting Hill Gate and demonstrated the impotence of female biceps in my attempts to crank it and been rescued by a taxi driver with a poor opinion of women, I asked nervously when I could have my final test and was told I had already passed it and could be posted to Station X2.

So, chaperoned by Daphne, who was inordinately relieved, I walked up the road one crisp clear morning, carrying Toddy's camping mattress, the army blanket, and the dogs' rug wrapped in an old mac and tied up with string. Daphne said I should need them to sleep on if I wanted to be really comfortable at night, for the hours of work had been changed so that we went on duty one morning at nine and didn't come off till nine am the next day, and then had forty-eight hours to recuperate. Daphne explained that this was perfectly lovely as it meant we should never have to walk to duty through what Mrs Dove called the barradge, which even Daphne found disagreeable.

'There,' said Daphne, pausing as we came in sight of X2, a great, ugly steel and concrete building taken over for the duration, standing in a section of road that had been blocked for weeks, 'look at us; we're still there and we've had twenty HEs within a hundred yards.'

Ignoring the Road Closed notice, we skirted a crater, strolled through the yard and went into the common room. It was an enormous place, with a concrete floor, where elegant cars had once stood, waiting smugly for purchasers. The huge plate-glass windows had long since been blown in, and they were boarded up so that most of the air and all the light was kept outside. In one corner, there was a meat safe hanging against the wall, above an oil-clothed table where an electric kettle stood on a tin tray beside an outsize brown tea-pot and a row of thick white cups. There was a ping-pong table under two bright lights, on which a cat was lazily playing with a cracked ball; a large green notice-board and a map with flags in it hung on the central wall, opposite to a rack filled with blankets and some shelves stuffed with rubber boots, and two rows of pegs with numbers on them. A few chairs were huddled beside radiators and a sagging, shabby couch stood by the one remaining window next to the dart-board. The floor was spotted with cigarette-ends and spilt ash; the room smelt of stale sweat and smoke. It wasn't surprising that the little group of men and women waiting by the door till the new shift took over looked pale and blank, as if they could hardly keep awake.

We lined up behind half a dozen women to sign the attendance book which was set on the nearest table.

The string on my bundle snapped, and the camping mattress caterpillared over the floor. The army blanket and the dogs' rug draped themselves over my feet.

Daphne said, 'Oh dear. I shall have to give you some luggage straps for Christmas. Kick them under the table and roll them up later when no one's looking.'

'Hallo, Penny,' said somebody, 'brought your new recruit?'

'At last,' said Daphne, who became Penny to me from that moment. 'You ought all to love me very much to-day because I've brought you such a marvellous new driver. She's taken a week learning to double-de-clutch at Central. But we'll forget that. Towser, Robin, Greeny, Johnny, Bill, Mark, meet Mrs Gibson.'

I blinked at them. As they turned to me, they were just a blur of faces under shabby peaked caps. They were kind and polite and a little wary. It was quite different from any ordinary social meeting. You can be a stranger at a cocktail party or a supper party, at a wedding breakfast or on a cruise, and be absorbed into the gathering in a few minutes. But though these people were glad to see you, ready to help you and show you around, you felt it would be ages before you belonged, that they had shared some experience together that made a bond closer than any ordinary liking, too strong to be broken by casual differences and irritations, and till you had shared it too, however long you spent with them, you would still be a stranger.

'Towser's our shift-leader,' said Penny. 'You want to watch your step with her.'

Towser laughed; she was square and dark, with a neat shingle that frothed into curls on her forehead; she had the slim sturdiness of a good hockey player, and it couldn't have been long since she was head girl somewhere. She said:

'Penny, you'd better be nice to your new girl. Maybe she'll give you a hand with morning cleaning.'

Penny said, 'Oh, Lor'. I'm not on cleaning *again*?'

There was a general movement towards the notice board. Grumbles bubbled up like froth on a glass of beer.

'Damn it, I'm on the phone at lunch …'

'Drat the woman, she's given me three patrols …'

'Oh, look here, it's not good enough. I swear I was on canteen last week. It's someone else's turn.'

'I guess,' said the one they called Robin, neat figured and fair, with raisin eyes, 'I guess I better put you wise and show you around. Penny's mind'll be all taken up with her cleaning. She's got her little apron on already.'

'Just hang up your hat and coat, darling,' said Penny, fluttering the strings of a short, stiff many-coloured apron which she wore to protect her best trousers. 'I'll explain everything presently.'

'That's the list of fatigues on the board now,' said Robin. 'And, oh boy, are there plenty of them? Soon Towser will put up the driving list and then you'll see what car you're on. Then you hang your tin hat and your gas mask on one of those pegs – they're numbered to match the cars. Drivers up top, attendants down below. We go two to an ambulance and the men mostly take the sitting-case cars. That stuff on the rail over there is gas clothing – not to be touched. Those are spare blankets for the ambulances – which reminds me, I got to check up on them. Got any knitting?'

I hadn't.

'I guess you'll be needing knitting,' said Robin. 'It passes the time.'

The morning began with cleaning; a good char would have made short work of it, but Penny and I blundered around, sweeping up and overlooking corners and going back to do them, and upsetting the dustpan and forgetting to empty ash trays and scrubbing over the tables and dusting what we could reach easily and leaving the rest. Two big doors at the far end of the room swung open to let in a current of cold air, till one of the men shining rubber boots in a corner shouted:

'Hi, Penny, you trying to give us pneumonia?'

The doors clamped shut, the wireless was turned on; somebody was giving a talk on cooking and nobody listened.

Towser came out from a cubby hole partitioned off in a corner and marked Control Room. She pinned another list on the board; people drifted up to look at it and drifted away again to hang their helmets on the appropriate peg and disappeared into the yard to clean their cars.

'The driver checks oil, water, lights and tyre pressure and cleans the coachwork,' said Robin. 'The attendant checks the equipment in the back and cleans that.'

'You're wanted in the Control Room, Mrs Gibson,' said Towser. 'The ASO – that's Auxiliary Station Officer – well, she's in.'

The tiny Control Room was cheerful; orange curtains framed the small window; bright posters hung on the walls, green painted bookshelves were crammed with files. The ASO was small and dark, in a neat tailored suit with three orange stripes on her arm. She smiled and thanked me for coming and hoped I would be happy, all in a gentle voice. I could draw my uniform that morning and would I just fill in a form?

Name … age … sex … address … Next of kin … Next of kin's telephone number if any … Religion.

'But *why* religion?'

'Just in case we have to bury you,' said the ASO.

'It's on the government,' said Towser cheerfully. 'Seven pound ten and a Union Jack. Just sign here.'

I wanted to ask if they had buried very many people, but it seemed indelicate.

The ASO said, 'By the way, I've found my cap.'

Towser said, 'Your cap? The one you lost the night your house went?'

She nodded solemnly. 'Remember how fussed I was about it? There was the house with no roof and cook under the table with the dinner service all over her, and all I could I worry about was my uniform cap. I kept saying but I must have my cap; it's LCC property, and if it's lost I've got to pay for it. Idiotic. And this morning, the woman who lives opposite brought it back to me. She found it in the middle of her dining-room table; it had been blown out of my house and across the road and in at her window.'

'What putrid luck about your house, though,' said Towser.

'But what good luck about my cap,' said the ASO.

Penny was waiting for me when we came out, with a large fat woman in tow; she wore a very tight blue uniform and a rather tight expression. Her trousers were too short.

'Mrs Boxer, our quartermaster,' said Penny. 'She's got your uniform here and there are …'

'Just a few forms to fill in,' I said.

Mrs Boxer.

Mrs Boxer beamed; evidently she enjoyed forms. 'I hope Mrs Gibson will be more careful of her uniform than you are, Penny,' said she. 'The coat is meant for wear, Mrs Gibson, not for wrapping round parcels. The badge should be kept clean and worn upon the right lapel, and not used for pinning up scarves. And you must understand that if you lose any of your equipment, except through enemy action, you are required to pay for it. Sign here, and here … and again here and here, please. There … the coat's not such a bad fit.'

The uniform was a little disappointing; the coat had to be several sizes too large for elegance, because, as it was cotton, you had to be padded with jerseys underneath. The cap had been

The uniform was a little disappointing.

worn by others before me and the brim was a little bent. But the tin hat with its white A on the front was comfortingly heavy and the gas mask reassuringly tight.

The whole morning was spent signing forms and fitting uniform and walking round the common room in my gas mask, with a post-card balanced on the container while I took deep breaths and hoped to hold it on by suction and so convince myself that I could go unscathed through the deadliest gas.

Then I spent an hour standing in the yard, looking at the petrol pumps, staring at the empty, gutted building opposite with its tattered advertisements of auction sales and old cinema shows, and hoping that someone would come in and have to be challenged and made to produce a pass. But no one did. Then it was time for lunch, and the long tables were pushed together and laid with dingy knives and forks and a hot meal appeared from a region I hadn't located.

In the afternoon, I was introduced to the ambulances; they stood in two rows in a covered yard, big saloons which had seen many a pleasure tour and were now fitted with large grey box bodies that held four stretchers and were closed with white canvas curtains that didn't quite meet.

'Easy to drive,' Penny said. 'Fords.'

'But why did I spend a week learning to drive that obsolete mammoth?' I said. 'I've driven Fords for a lifetime.'

'They don't behave quite the same with these bodies on,' said Penny. 'You've got to mind your corners or you'll spill your patients. Come on in now and have a sit-down. There won't be an alert to-day. Too clear.'

There wasn't an alert that night either. As the hours crawled by, I saw what Robin meant about the knitting. My carefully screwed up courage simmered into peevishness, till I was almost indignant at wasting a white night that could have been spent in a proper bed, sitting on a deck chair that pinched my thighs, while half the shift dozed stiffly in corners or snored on stretchers slung between two chairs or pushed into the shadow of a table.

Most of the girls had tied their hair up in fishnet scarves or silk handkerchiefs. Two of them even greased their hands and put on old white gloves. Penny had her own ritual of changing her best trousers and hanging them carefully on a chair in the upstairs cloakroom to preserve the crease, while she pulled on a shabby pair of corduroys which didn't mind being pushed into a sleeping bag. Nearly all of them had arranged a makeshift bedside table, setting out cough drops, torch, aspirin, novel and water in a cracked cup on the floor beside them, or on a chair or an upturned packing-case. It gave them the illusion of going properly to bed.

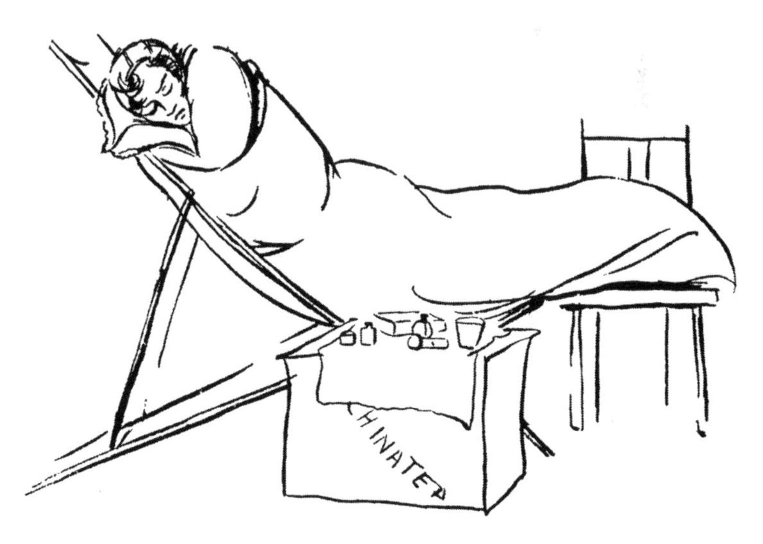

A makeshift bedside table.

'Two-thirty and thank God,' said Penny at last. 'Our turn to rest now. I've bagged two stretchers. Under the ping-pong table. It's not too draughty and it's out of the light. You'll sleep there.'

I did.

During the next week or two, the weather was baddish and though the sirens usually went off about seven, the raids were on a smaller scale, or at any rate, they were much less severe in our district.

There were no excitements at work, and on our free evenings, Penny and I and Belinda would sit in the drawing- room, reading and writing letters, and sometimes Penny and Belinda would pick up tin hats and go out and have a look for incendiaries.

'They sound like a lot of old pans falling down,' said Penny. 'But often you don't hear them. That's the trouble.'

This was the time when incendiaries were like small fireworks and not much more dangerous. There was no explosive charge, and if we hadn't, all of us, actually put them out ourselves, we all knew people who had got the better of them with stirrup pumps and sand, basins and tin hats, or even by jumping on them – though this was bad for the shoes.

Penny and Belinda really hoped to find one in the back garden, but they never did. They would come back looking important and say, 'I'm afraid the East End's getting it again,' or, 'There's trouble south of the river.' Or, 'Oh dear, there's a big fire away to the north.' They spoke restlessly and prowled about the room, tidying things away, and you could see that they hated to think of other parts of London being hurt while they sat at home.

Sometimes the siren would go as usual, and then there'd be an All Clear, just as you'd got to sleep, and then another siren, just as you were dreaming. That annoyed all of us, but especially Mrs Dove, who always tramped purposefully up to the attic at the All Clear, only to be fetched down again at the next alert.

'Come down at once, Mrs Dove,' Penny used to shout upstairs. 'It'd be much too much trouble to rescue you from the attic.'

And Mrs Dove would come down, breathing resentfully, dressed in a siren suit, a clean apron and a short fur coat and carrying her best hat and a smart dressing-bag.

'What do they think they're doing with them sireens?' she'd say. 'Giving us a concert? Waking up honest folk – it oughtn't to be allowed.'

And once the sirens never went at all, and Belinda and I spent the evening wallowing in hot baths, instead of splashing hurriedly in and out, largely to please Penny, who said regularly every night at bedtime: 'But of *course* you must have a bath, Mildred. There's nothing to be nervous of in a *bath*. Everyone knows they always land right side up in the road with you inside.'

That blessed night, we went to sleep in real soft beds, between clean sheets, in our own rooms, where we could snore or cough or roll about without apologising, flopping back on the pillows with a sigh of such deep content that it was almost a prayer of thanksgiving in itself, slipping at once into the quiet sleep that tasted better than any banquet, was more prized than any fortune.

Next day, half London said to the other half, 'What a *lovely* night.'

At the Station, nothing much seemed to happen. I learned how to fold blankets, how to make intensely strong tea when the men shouted, 'Tea up, tea up, girls.' And how to swab the floor of an ambulance without leaving my own footprints behind, how to play darts, how to say gravely, 'Station X2,' when I answered the phone, and how to distinguish between a strange body called Group, which co-ordinated the Ambulance Stations of several boroughs, and Central, which administered them, and Report and Control, which was the nerve centre for all the ARP services of the borough, from which all calls for ambulances came, and which was forever sending messages about the capacity of hospitals for casualties, requiring to be told our state of parties, or checking the line or informing us that there was an Air Raid Message Yellow, Red, Purple or White. I learned how to do double knitting, how to cope with a document called a case sheet which had to be filled in whenever an ambulance left the station, and on which speedometer readings had to be recorded whatever else was not, how to play ping-pong, how to tell the time by the twenty-four hour clock, and how to play more ping-pong.

Some days an earnest gentleman would come to lecture on gas, and we recited the Order of Dressing and Undressing, like four-year-olds chanting the two-times table, beginning always with the cry, 'Attend to the Wants of Nature.' We sniffed repulsive little phials of lethal gases and were invariably asked when we would assume the respirator if called to a gas incident. Invariably, we said, 'On leaving the Station'; invariably we were told that this was not correct; we ought to say, 'When the presence of gas is detected.'

'Say,' asked Robin, 'what if a gas bomb hits the ambulance?'

'Oh, come now,' said the lecturer, brushing this aside as a frivolous question, 'how many times have ambulances been hit?'

'We did not know – but we all wanted to. We weren't quite satisfied when he said, 'Hardly ever.'

Twice an instructor came down from Central, to give me another driving test, to make sure that I could handle a Ford. Once an instructor came down from Central to see if I could drive an ambulance in a gas-mask, and once I drove all the way to Central in the dark on a rainy night, to take a test to make sure that I could drive an ambulance in the dark on a rainy night. As the siren went when I got there, I never took the test.

Slowly, I got to know about the other people on the station, for Penny knew all their life stories and told them to me in instalments. Most of the men had served in the last war; between wars, they had been mechanics and taxi-drivers, chauffeurs and commercial travellers. They called us by our nicknames; they liked to be asked to back our ambulances into position, and they helped with the fatigues and played ping-pong with us. But when it came to conversation, they preferred their own, and in the long evenings, they sat beside the wireless, playing draughts and grumbling gently about grievances which they forgot the minute an alert went.

Some of the women had been on the Station from the beginning of the war, when their ordinary jobs had shown signs of packing up. Robin had been a journalist – hence her American twang: Johnny had been a mannequin, which was why her hair frothed so charmingly round her forehead and lay like a little girl's curls on the collar of the tailored suit she had got herself through the trade. Greeny was a tough middle-aged woman who had run a hat shop; she still made a penny or two on the side, altering our old felts, and when things were quiet, she was often in the upstairs cloakroom, screwing her neck nearly off to judge the sit of a hat in the spotted glass. Bill, who looked too small and frail to crank a car or lift a patient, had been a governess; she was really stronger than any of us, and had a way of pushing out her chin and shouldering a couple of stretchers as if they had been walking-sticks.

They were all very polite and very kind. Robin would say, 'Pull in, Mrs Gibson, and park your feet on the radiator.' And in the evenings, Mark, who was Penny's special crony, a still, quiet person, with a pale face under smooth gold hair, would say, 'Come on, Mrs Gibson, bring your bit of sausage over here and we'll have some china tea together.'

I was Mrs Gibson to them, and they were Miss Robinson and Mrs Markston and Miss Billings and Mrs Green to me.

Mostly, I listened while they talked, and mostly they talked of the early days of the blitz, partly, I used to think, because they liked to toughen a newcomer, but even more because those shared nights of flame and ruin had forged a bond between them that was renewed every time they remembered.

'Just fancy,' said Penny, one night, 'it's weeks since we've been out.'

'Makes me mad,' said Robin, 'to think of Coventry.'

'I'd almost sooner they stuck to London,' Mark said. 'After all, we're used to it. All the rats have gone now and only people who can take it are left.'

'Remember our first trip?' said Robin. 'Oh boy, that was a night. When Mark and I went to that blaze up the street behind? And the warden said he guessed we'd do better to park round the next corner.'

'I never knew,' said Mark, 'why I moved on. I didn't mean to.'

'There wasn't much left of that corner we stopped at first,' said Robin.

'We popped into the back of the ambulance when we heard that one coming, just like a couple of scared rabbits.'

'We sure felt silly, when we came to, squatting on the floor, holding hands.'

'It's all luck,' said Mark. 'At least …'

'Remember the night Clovelly Court went? And Penny brought in the little kid who cried all night. Said her mother was beetroot.'

'… and all those people who came and parked themselves on the men's sofa and wouldn't move till daylight?'

'… and the little boy who howled because he'd nothing on but his vest? And the row there was because we lost the blanket we gave him?'

'… the night Bill was out seven hours and Penny had to massage her feet in the morning because she was so cold?'

'… and then they never got the casualty out. It was all for nothing …'

'… the night at the Middlesex when a bread-basket came down … all those incendiaries, popping down between the ambulances and not one was touched …'

'… she kept saying, "Don't worry about me, dearie, I'm all right." And when we got her to hospital, we saw something had ripped her guts out.'

'I'm almost more afraid of being sick than of anything,' said Penny.

I pushed my plate away.

IV December, 1940

One cold, frosty Sunday in December, when it hurt our chilblained hands to clean the ambulances, and we stamped up and down on patrol, wearing fleece-lined boots if we could borrow them, and our own overcoats over the cotton uniforms, shivering with cold and boredom, things did happen.

The toe of her oiled wool sock flapped as she put her boots on.

The sirens went early; the men had only just finished putting up the blackout. Johnny and Bill were first ambulance out. Johnny swore and put away the fragile chiffon nightgown she was embroidering, wrapping it tenderly in tissue paper and old linen, before she tramped across the room and got her coat and her tin hat and gas mask from the peg. She leaned up against the wall to put on her rubber boots; the toe of her oiled wool sock flapped ridiculously, and her fair hair fell forward over her flushed face till she straightened and tucked her curls under her helmet. Bill stuck out her chin, lit a cigarette and went to the Control room, got a case sheet and pencil, a hooded torch and a map and parked them on the floor beside her canvas chair; then she went on with the crossword she was doing.

'An obsolete mammal in five letters?' she murmured.

Penny and I were playing ping-pong. There was no reason to stop; she was last out with Mark, and I was fourth with Robin. It was a noisier alert than usual; the angry guns barked continuously; the wireless programme faded out and every now and then there was a crump that brought little jets of dust spurting from the shutters and the sandbags.

Penny and I went on playing ping-pong.

Three men outside, on patrol and watching for incendiaries, suddenly ran in and fell flat on their faces. A boot fell off a shelf and the lights swung backwards and forwards and I missed Penny's serve.

'My game,' said Penny. 'Like another?'

I nodded. But I didn't really mean it. Something odd was happening to my stomach; it felt as swollen as a barrage balloon and if I hadn't had heavy shoes on, I believe I'd have gone up to the ceiling.

'We'll be out before long,' said Mark. She sat in an easy chair, not knitting or reading, her hands just loosely clasped, and a queer, almost exultant look on her face.

The building shivered like a feverish patient; the walls seemed to close in; the ceiling, with its great girders, seemed to press on one's head. That awful rat of cowardice was gnawing at my guts again, and my hands were so damp I dropped the ping-pong bat.

'Ten all,' said Penny. 'I'll take this game too if you aren't careful.' She was smiling, and her eyes were lit with courage: she looked so young it was impossible to believe in those grandchildren in the country.

When the phone went, the very ping-pong ball seemed to hang suspended in mid-air as we all turned to listen. My bowels seemed to drop right out; I felt I couldn't have moved a step even if I'd had a pistol at my back. Across the hush in the room, we could hear the shift-leader taking down particulars about the capacity of hospitals.

The ASO came in; she went to the notice board and looked at the lists, spoke to Johnny and Bill and asked Mark to play billiards.

'Nothing much doing at present,' she said.

'They mean business all right,' said the man on patrol. 'Dropping flares all over, they are.'

'Has anyone got the key of the downstairs lavatory?' asked Penny in a resonant whisper. 'We aren't allowed to go to the upstairs one in bad blitz,' she explained to me.

'Not since the day Penny was blown off the lavatory seat,' said Mark, chalking her cue. 'Remember, Penny? When they hit the flats just behind and you shot out on your hands and knees and fell downstairs, pulling up your pants?'

'I never did get my pants zipped up that day,' said Penny. 'I felt quite uncomfortable.'

Mark went back to her billiards and made a break of 850.

I heard the unmistakable double drone of enemy aircraft overhead as the ASO cannoned neatly off the red.

'They're after that damn' place up the road,' said Johnny, referring to our local military objective.

'I wish to hell they'd hit it and go home,' said Robin.

I looked at my watch; it was only nine and the raid had been on three hours, with spasms of noise and moments of deceptive quiet. When Penny said it was like having a baby, I knew just what she meant. Even she was tired of ping-pong now and I dared not knit because I would drop stitches.

'You'd better have supper while you have the chance,' said Mark. I got out a lump of cold pie and ate it in my fingers where I stood, hoping that at least it would weight down my stomach. Mark and Penny began methodically to lay a little tray for themselves, with a pretty paper cloth, watercress in a glass bowl and cold boiled bacon and pickles.

The shift-leader went out to have a look at the night and came back to have a look at me, rather as if I were an unreliable centre forward in a hockey match.

'You ought to lie down, you know,' she said. 'You're supposed to be resting, and you mightn't be out till two or three tomorrow, if then. No need to get excited.'

I said I'd lie down.

'By the way,' she added, 'I just thought I'd warn you – you do know we're not supposed to carry corpses, don't you?'

Mark turned round from her supper and spoke with her mouth full. 'You want to be careful about that,' she said. 'I got landed with a body once … couldn't get rid of it …'

Mrs Boxer, the quartermaster, came in, explaining volubly that she'd just looked in to see if her stores were all right. 'One or two little things to see to,' she said. 'Just one or two little things.'

She caught sight of me. 'Ah, Mrs Gibson, I thought you were on to-night. This form isn't quite correct … do you mind if we get it right? I like to have everything cut and dried.'

I asked what was wrong with the form and fumbled for my fountain pen.

'Your next of kin,' she said. 'You've given someone right up in Scotland.'

'That is my next of kin.'

'But we'll have to have another; someone nearer; a friend in London would do. Just to identify remains, you know. We couldn't possibly wait for someone to come down from Scotland to identify. You do see my point? It's so important to have things cut and dried.'

I made her happy with the name of my solicitor and took a stretcher over to the radiators. Robin was already dozing in a deck chair, with a rug over her knees, snoring gently. She was an experienced traveller and probably a bad raid was no more to her than a Channel crossing. The hot water sizzling in the pipes counterfeited the sound of aircraft, at any rate, you couldn't tell which was which. Presently hot dinner for the men appeared; I wondered who had cooked that hot joint and that steamed pudding. The men put down their pipes and cigarettes and sat down to it.

The spatter of knives and forks, the querk of someone's hiccups, the sizzling of the water, Robin's uneasy snore, they made a queer, comforting pattern of homely sound against the hellish orchestra of guns and bombs outside.

The men pushed back their chairs and shouted, 'Tea up. Tea up. Tea up.'

Greeny put aside the hat she was altering and got up to make it, tossing her head.

The telephone went: the shift-leader shot to it : 'Station X2 … one ambulance, one car to the junction of … and … Message received, 22.43.'

Johnny and Bill were on their feet; Bill ran out to her car and one of the men went with her. Johnny waited, case sheet in hand, for final instructions. Greeny went on making tea. I watched them go.

Over the door was a notice I hadn't seen till then:

Be Careful
A Cat Has Nine Lives; You Have Only One.

The phone went again; Robin woke instantly. 'Better get ready, dear,' she said.

Another ambulance and another car went off as I pulled on my boots and my coat and my gas mask and my tin hat and pushed my fingers into my gloves.

'We're off,' said Robin, as another call came through. 'Take the ambulance that's standing first, start it up and I'll join you.'

The dim blue light in the yard made the sky behind seem almost green; it was pallid with flame; the smell of explosives and charred timber and crumbling masonry was like the stench of hell.

I got into my ambulance because I had been told to do it, because I belonged to a generation brought up to obey orders. If I hadn't been, I expect I'd have run away.

Robin suddenly appeared, snapped open the door and got in.

'First left, dear, and then straight,' she said. 'I know the way.'

I yanked at the lever, rasping it into bottom gear, and we jerked off.

'There,' said Robin, 'I darn well forgot to take the speedometer reading. Guess I can fix it later.'

We turned into the straight. 'Bright, isn't it?' said Robin. 'We can sure see.'

'We can see,' I said.

'Somehow,' said Robin irrelevantly as we rumbled down the broad road, 'I've an idea these little flat hats aren't going to suit me. Maybe I'd look better in a high crown.'

'M-m-much b-b-better in a high c-c-crown,' I said.

There was a fantastic façade of flame ahead; weird shadows criss-crossed the street, and now and then, at a near explosion, the whole sky opened and shut and a wall of white light came walking down the street to meet us. We turned a corner and were enveloped in thick fog; red lights wavered through it, and a bell began to ring.

'Road blocked,' said Robin. 'I'll get out and see you back.'

She got out; she stood in the middle of the road, directing me with sure, unhurried gestures. I knew then how much you could love people when you'd been through the blitz with them.

We backed and turned and made a detour and pulled up at a point where the fog was even thicker, the air almost solid with powdered debris. There had been a heavy bomb.

Robin got out again; she sniffed and reached into the dashboard cubby hole for a couple of mica eye shields.

'May as well have them handy,' she said. 'There's plenty of smoke. I'll find a warden. Shan't be long.'

But she seemed to be away a long time. It was very dark; yet when you looked up, you could see that beyond the blanket of fog, the sky was ominously bright. When I switched off the engine – and I hated switching off the engine because then I let in the drone of planes overhead – there was a soft slurring sound, with a crackling undertone like the noise of footsteps in crisp snow or crunched ice. I got out to see what it was, and immediately my own boots rustled over broken glass. Dim figures were straggling across the road, arms round each other's shoulders, limping and swaying. They were the walking casualties, going to the First Aid Post across the way. It was odd to see so many of them, creeping from the ruins, in that street which seemed to smell of death.

Just as Robin came back, there was a sharp crack and the gloom lifted: a couple of streets away, a firework of blue and green and gold sprayed upwards.

'Gas,' said Robin. 'And don't fuss with your gas-mask, dear. That's a house main: I'd sooner see it than smell it.'

I tried to look as if my hand hadn't panicked towards my respirator and Robin told me to drive round the block as they were bringing casualties out at the other end of the street; a house had fallen right across the road at this one.

We rounded a couple of corners and were back at the burglar alarm. It rang crazily at the sight of us. This time, Robin got out and stepped over the barrier, strolled down the street fifty yards and came back to say that we could make it: a couple of ambulances had gone down already.

As we crept down the road, the bell ringing so crazily that it seemed sacrilegous to deny it, one wheel jolting against the kerb, the other bumping over rubble at the edge of a small crater, a warden came up and got on the running board. He had a casualty waiting for us, a woman who was bed-ridden on the top floor of a house whose roof had been blown off. The place was in an alley, so narrow that we nearly took away the lamp-post at the corner.

Outside the house, we waited again. A warden in the white hat of great authority spoke to Robin.

The glass was over my ankles when I got out to give a hand with the stretcher. We slid it off the runners and set it on the pavement complete with blankets. The stretcher party would bring their own and take ours away, for blankets and stretchers were interchangable.

The warden went into the house. Robin followed.

'You stay by the ambulance,' she said. 'That's your job. I'll yell if we want you.'

I waited in the doorway, where I could keep an eye on both Robin and the ambulance. The warden's hoarse voice echoed down the stairs.

'You girls stick below. 'Tisn't a job for you.'

I turned then, and saw that at the bend in the narrow stairs, the side of the house was missing; the ricketty steps went up, like a ladder across a crevasse, to the landing above.

The stretcher party arrived, the leader wearing a white hat marked SP, and went straight up.

A door behind us opened, and a very small woman came out. She was wearing her Sunday hat with feathers in it, and little fur tippet; she carried a very worn broom.

'I'm sorry you should see the house in such a state,' she said, shaking her head at us. 'I don't like you ladies to see the house in such a state, but there, you can't do much cleaning up till morning, can you?'

She swept a clutter of glass and plaster forcefully into the gutter and popped back into her room.

'The wardens'll be after her, poor soul,' said Robin. 'I don't suppose the house is safe, but I bet she won't want to leave it.'

'I don't like you ladies to see the house in such a state.'

The stretcher party came down; somehow they eased their burden round the turn in the stairs where the wall had gone, and somehow they spared breath to talk to the patient.

'There you are, mother,' said the leader. 'You're all right. Fresh as a daisy you'll be, come tomorrow.'

Robin got into the back of the ambulance as the handles of the stretcher slid on to the runners. The fog had lifted and I could see the old woman's patient face, so thickly coated with fine white dust that she looked like a living plaster cast.

I got into the driving seat and started up; it was nice to hear the engine spluttering again; it deadened other noises that one didn't want to hear. The hatch in the wooden partition at my back clicked open to frame Robin's face.

'Know your way to hospital? Take it easy. She's badly shocked.'

There was a T junction at the end of the alley. As I hesitated, a rescue man, overalls whitened with dust, came up.

'Where d'you want to go to, mate?'

I told him.

'Can't get through to the right. It's chest 'igh in derbis. I'll see you out the other way.'

There was plenty of debris in the other alley too: a couple of shutters and some battered furniture had been blown into the road. The rescue man obligingly moved the worst of it for me.'

'You'll be OK now,' he said, waving me on.

I drove out into a broad street, clear of smoke. All along it red lights winked, marking craters or fallen masonry. But it wasn't empty. Police cars, ARP cars, stretcher party cars, AFS cars, fire engines and trailer pumps, these legitimately usurped the road. And a string of private cars, recklessly driven, flicked in and out among them, the cars of people who had been dining and wining and dancing in the West End when the raid caught them and were now crazily racing home.

It was quieter by the hospital; an ambulance drove off just as we reached it, and a couple of elderly bearers in baize aprons and tin hats came down the steps. I went and stood opposite to Robin to help take the weight as the men eased the stretcher out. Then I sat in the ambulance and waited for Robin to deliver her patient and collect two more blankets and another stretcher to replace the ones we'd left.

'Sorry to keep you,' she said. 'They tried to put me off with one blanket. What a nerve! You got to look out for that sort of thing. If we were a blanket short tomorrow, oh boy, what a raspberry we'd get from Mrs Boxer.'

'Home now?' I said.

'Home, James. We don't have to report back.'

I drove quickly away.

'Just imagine,' said Robin, 'that poor soul's left her bag with all her bits and pieces in it behind. Wonder if there's a hope of getting it for her. Said I'd try tomorrow. Maybe, if I went down, first thing ...'

Driving into the yard of Station X2 was like making port after a storm at sea. I leaned back, suddenly happy, and watched Robin peering at the speedometer reading. Then she went to make her report and I handed over the ambulance to the OC cars before I followed her.

The shift-leader and the ASO were filling in forms as if victory depended on it. All our doings for the night had to be entered in the Occurrence Book and in triplicate on forms.

The ASO looked up to say, 'Everything all right?'

'OK,' said Robin.

'Have a cigarette. You too, Mrs Gibson. So you've been blooded. Feel all right?'

'I feel fine,' I said, and was surprised that it was true.

The ASO gave us her nice warm smile that made the Control Room seem a homely place to come back to. Then she got busy on the case sheet.

'Is it complete? Time of call: 23.45 … leaving station, 23.47. Arrival at incident?'

'Call it 00.5,' said Robin. 'Didn't think to look at my watch.'

'Time of return, 01.50. Speedometer reading on outward trip … you didn't note it?'

'I'll fix it with the OC cars,' said Robin quickly.

'Number of casualties carried … 1 female. Sign it, will you? Then go and have a rest. You may be out again any time.'

There was a shout of 'Tea up. Tea up, girls,' as we left the Control Room, and a little crowd began to collect round the big brown teapot, where Greeny was making tea, just as she had been when we left, only now she had her helmet and coat on.

Men and women lined up together, holding out their cups and talking.

'Have a good trip?'

'Pansy.'

'Down the road … to pick up a fireman … badly burned … poor devil.'

'... out at the back here ... old man with a broken thigh ... joked all the way ...'

They turned as we came in, put down their cups and hailed us.

'Hallo Robin, you all right? Been gone a long time.'

'Hallo, Gibsy! Want your tea?'

'How'd you get on, Gibsy? Enjoy yourself?'

'Come near the radiators, Gibsy, and warm yourself up.'

'So far,' said Mark thoughtfully, 'it's been a pretty quiet night.'

'It's not over yet,' said Greeny.

But so far as we were concerned, it was over. When Penny and I went out to fetch water from the tap in the yard an hour later, it was suddenly and blessedly raining: the sky was dimmed with cloud, and already the flames were turning to smoke. Penny and I just stood there, holding each other's hands, as we looked up at it.

The All Clear went at two: we seemed to feel the whole city relax a little as we tugged off our boots, dropping them where we stood, and flopped on to stretchers, falling at once into the depths of sleep.

When we woke, the wireless was announcing that London had experienced a sharp raid, and the early patrol had got hold of a paper which carried the headline: London's Coventry.

'*How* they exaggerate,' said Mark. 'It's *quite* ridiculous.'

There was a smell of bacon, an exquisite wave of it, and breakfast mysteriously appeared. I made a note to find out from Penny whence and how it came and whether any raid had ever disconcerted the canteen cook.

As we were eating, a woman warden appeared in the doorway. I was officially on patrol, so I got up and challenged her.

'Someone from this Station reported an unexploded bomb at 23.57 last night,' she said. 'I should like all particulars. I must ascertain its precise locality.'

She had obviously been out all night; her voice was tonelessly determined; she stooped a little, as if her helmet were too heavy for her. But she would not go till she had cross-questioned

Towser and everyone else on the Station at the time. When we offered her breakfast, she shook her head.

'I would sooner ascertain its precise locality first,' she said.

'Gee,' said Robin, reaching for the marmalade. 'I'll say those wardens have a tougher time than we do.'

A woman warden appeared. She had obviously been out all night.

V December, 1940

After that night, I began to feel differently about the blitz. I was never so frightened again, because I was never alone in it any more: I was one of a vast army of women, going into action in all the shattered towns, whether they drove through raids, or answered telephones, or worked at First Aid Posts or on canteens, or whether they just stayed at home and endured it. It was almost like being part of a composite personality; their courage was your courage, their danger – yours.

And then, too, when you looked around, you saw how much worse it was for other people; firemen and wardens and doctors and nurses, they all had a far tougher job than ours to do, and every single civilian, bowler-hatted city man, lovely blonde in her mink coat, housewife, workman, dustman, tramp, any of them might have to endure pain and horror any night of the week. You found yourself looking at them, as they went about, and though they were strangers, they became important to you; suddenly they were all of them lovable. Not likeable – you never could like very many people. But you could love them, even if you didn't know you were doing it. Certainly, you loved them directly they became a casualty, for then they represented a life to be saved, a life for which wardens and rescue men, stretcher-bearers, police, ambulance crews, doctors and nurses would unhesitatingly risk their own. The life might have no importance in economic terms; it might be a shiftless, meaningless life, of no apparent value to the community, a life which any conference of hard-headed economists or eugenists would consider wasteful and unprofitable and better lost. But to the ARP services, it was a life, a human creature. Even while they dug and sweated in the rubble, that life was important and that stranger became a personal friend. Every elderly man was 'Dad', every ageing woman 'Mother', and all the others, Mate, or Sister, Son or Darling.

It was queer, and strangely comforting, that in the midst of all that destruction we set so much value on a single life that a dozen would be risked to save it, and yet we set so little value on life that we would risk twelve valuable, healthy, skilled lives for one old woman of ninety, one paralysed child, or even, sometimes, for a cat or a dog. Perhaps that was just why we won the battles of London, Bristol, Coventry and the rest.

At any rate, this queer, unfamiliar feeling of loving people whether you knew them or not made the blitz bearable. It really wasn't bearable if you tried to meet it with defiance. 'The Huns aren't going to get me down', 'Hitler shan't break my nerve', these slogans didn't take one far. It wasn't much use, either, comforting yourself with statistics and working out the chances of being hit in a house or a shelter or in the street or driving a car and telling yourself that with luck, you would be alive with the great majority. And somehow, the fatalistic 'I'm not worrying; I guess my bit's got my name on it,' didn't do either, though most of the men seemed to take to it.

At least, it wasn't enough if you were much of a coward. And, fortunately for me, I was just too much of a coward to get along by pretending to be tough. For one thing, it was no use fighting fear: the more you tried to control the rumblings of your stomach and the shaking of your hands and the quaking of your knees, the more you rumbled and shook and quaked. You only broke free from fear when you broke free from yourself and minded more about other people.

I remember Mark, who was just about the calmest and steadiest person on the Station, saying how sick she had felt on her first trip. She'd had to go to an incident in one of the Parks, and as she drove through the filthy, smoky dimness, she met an elderly warden, cycling along by himself from one incident to another. And she thought:

'There's that poor little man, out in it alone, with only a bike, and I'm in this comfortable ambulance and somebody with me. If he isn't afraid, I've no right to be.'

And Penny, whose first call was to a fire, where she collected a fireman with a broken leg, always said that she stood beside him in the ambulance with her teeth chattering so loudly that he heard. He said, 'You got the wind up?' And she said, 'I'm absolutely terrified,' and he said, 'That's OK. You'll be quite all right.' He laughed and joked all the way to hospital, and she was so touched because he was kind that she quite forgot to be afraid. As far as I know, she's never remembered since.

So we got in the way of thinking of all the people who were in much greater danger than we were, and when the sirens went, subconsciously we turned our minds to all these others, so that our hearts went out to the little broken homes, to the women and children and old men and boys prisoned under debris, frightened and trapped. Then nothing mattered except getting there to help.

Some of us, the old-fashioned ones, perhaps, prayed for these people and so forestalled our own fear. Most of us, I believe, prayed without knowing what we did, so that sometimes the very oaths that burned on our lips were really prayers.

Only Penny had been known to say, outrageously, as she drove down a narrow street between two fires: 'D'you mind if I say my prayers?'

And the man who was with her said, 'Carry on, Penny.'

So, instead of dreading a call, we all longed to be out on the job, and the most trying nights were those when raids were bad and yet there was nothing we could do because the bombs in our district brought no casualties. The night the City burned, I was first ambulance out with Penny; we kept on going out into the yard and simply staring at that solid bastion of flame; again and again, we revved the car up to make sure it would start, and every time the telephone went, we stood tiptoe at the Control Room door. But the City burned, and there was no job for us; we waited in the yard, Penny, Mark, Greeny and I, and watched it in tears.

For a little time after that Sunday raid, the pace at which we lived quickened unbearably. Already we were almost painfully aware of living; getting up, to see the thin line of daylight under the shutters, to feel cool lino under one's feet, to sniff the rare smell of a good stew, to see the twigs, etched dark against the sky, swelling already in the hope of spring, to hear the sound of cats squirling and dirling in the garden at twilight. The feel of one's head on a pillow, the caress of sleep, every sensation was pitched up. Now we were goaded on by an uneasy memory of all the things we might have done better and quicker when the emergency came.

'We don't know nearly enough,' Penny said, her face puckered with distress, as we sat round the telephone table having mid-morning coffee at the Station. 'I had to stop to ask my way to the hospital the other night. We must do more topography …'

'It'd be so awful,' said Johnny, putting away her fine sewing and picking up a Red Cross book, 'if we made a mistake. Supposing you couldn't find a pressure point … I dream about it sometimes …'

'It's loading that gets me down,' said Greeny.

'If they use gas …' said Mark, 'we ought to do hard work in our gas masks …'

'Incendiaries,' I said, 'I've never seen one yet.'

'Blankets,' snapped Mrs Boxer. 'And eye shields. There are three eye shields missing. Supposing you were called to a fire to-night …'

'Procedure,' insisted the ASO. 'We ought to know it. Gibsy, do you know a senior warden from an incident officer?'

'A fractured femur,' murmured Johnny '"pad under the armpit, long splint, eight bandages … which goes first"?'

'Come and be a broken back, lumbar region, Gibsy, I want to load you face downwards …'

'Who knows the quickest way to St Andrew's, Dollis Hill?'

'Is it BBC you confuse with mustard? Is it paste or ointment for Lewisite?' said Mark.

'A white hat and one stripe …' said the ASO.

'… loading in the Fowler position for an abdominal …'

'How'd you load an abdominal if its back were broken too?' asked Penny nervously.

'In the mortuary van,' said Robin.

'Gas cleansing stations, decontamination of men and vehicles …'

'You could quite easily get to know your wardens in your spare time,' insisted the ASO. 'Gibsy, I think you ought to …'

'Go to the pub and you'll get to know our district warden,' put in Robin. 'He keeps it.'

'No, seriously, Gibsy,' said the ASO, who liked to carry her point. 'In your hour off to-day ... go round to the post. You should. After all, you do know less than the others.'

The post was in the basement of a largish house that also stocked a Red Cross office and some WVS people. You went through a garden that had been trim and pretty before all the beds had been trampled into a sticky mess, down some rather slippery steps into an area, where you stumbled over a cat, dodged round the sandbags and went in to what had once been somebody's scullery. There was a kettle simmering on a gas ring, and a nice big tea-pot and some variegated tea cups on a shelf. The passage was the usual imitation of something out of a coal mine, and the main room was pit-propped too. There were half a dozen deck chairs grouped round an electric fire, the usual pick-axe and saw hung on the wall beside fire buckets and a couple of stirrup pumps. A very large map of the sector, with flags stuck in it to mark Fire Stations, First Aid Posts and the places where bombs had fallen hung over the fireplace, so that everyone who wanted a close-up of it must have singed their trousers.

At the telephone, talking purposefully to Report and Control who were engaged in their nightly recital of hospitals, receiving capacity of, was the little woman warden who had come about an unexploded bomb. She must have been nearer sixty than fifty, I thought, now I had time to look at her. Beside her on the table was a shiny black bag, out of which stuck some knitting, a couple of exercise books and a thermos flask. Evidently she mistrusted ARP tea.

'I say,' I said. 'Did you find it?'

'Find what?'

'Our bomb. Our unexploded bomb,' I said. It seemed impossible that she could have forgotten such an important thing as our unexploded bomb.

'Oh, you're from Station X2, are you? I don't think you need worry about your bomb. I failed to locate it, but that is because it was incorrectly reported. No doubt, in the confusion –'

'There wasn't any confusion,' I said indignantly.

'It is not always possible to be sure of direction in the … er … heat of the moment. Your ASO probably heard a distant explosion. Or even a time bomb. I located a time bomb quite near you, but my difficulty is that its position doesn't coincide with your report.'

I said quickly that the time bomb would do very nicely and what, anyway, was the difference between a time bomb and an unexploded bomb?

'You know a time bomb *will* go off,' she said. 'Whereas you can justifiably hope that an unexploded bomb will not.'

'But how do you know which is which?' I asked.

She went into technicalities. Her prim, academic voice contrasted eerily with the pictures of chaos and drama the words called up. Time bombs were smaller, it seemed, because the idea was that you didn't notice the slight mess they made and let them go off while you were still getting on with your job. Whereas an unexploded bomb might weigh anything from twenty pounds to a ton, in which case someone would certainly notice the hole.

'You would expect to find a small well-marked crater,' she said, ' with little surrounding damage. There is very little blast, you see, and of course, no fragmentation.'

I said I quite saw and made a note to have a look in Penny's garden, just to make sure she and Belinda had not overlooked any small, well-marked craters.

'That Sunday night must have been pretty awful, wasn't it?' I said. 'For you people, I mean?'

'Rather busy,' she said.

'You were out in it?' I said.

'I did my patrols. We have a rota, you know.'

I nodded; I understood about rotas. Like strong tea, they are inseparable from ARP. I knew, without being told, that the Post had a rota for patrols, for telephone duty, for sleeping, for getting tea, for washing up and for sweeping the floor. Just as we did.

'It's quite a simple organisation, you see,' she said, beginning to explain it. 'At this post we've got a post warden over us, and we're responsible for all the streets within the red line on the map; it doesn't look a great deal, but if a couple of bombs drop, it can entail considerable work. The district warden is in charge of several posts, and he is under the chief warden, who is responsible for the Borough. There are also wardens on special work at the Town Hall.'

'We don't have anything to do with the Town Hall,' I said. 'Unless Report and Control live there.'

'You're LCC, and we're Borough,' said the warden. 'Report and Control really links us up. Round about here we don't have many paid wardens – most of us are voluntary.'

'Night duty after a full day's work?' I said.

'Three nights a week,' she said. 'I teach at the Polytechnic. Book-keeping. Here we do from 5–12 or 12–7.'

'Always on patrol? All that time? Out in it, for seven or eight hours on end?'

'Dear me, no. If it's a quietish night, there are two or three of us on, and we take it in turns to be on watch. Sometimes we go upstairs; the landing window commands a very adequate view of the sector, since the flats over the way went. We do two or three patrols as well, of course. Earlyish for lights … And then we turn out later on, just to make sure.'

'And if it's a bad night,' I said, 'like Sunday?'

'Then we're patrolling most of the time – if it's our turn by the rota. In fact, we expect to be occupied all night.'

'The worse it is, the more you're out?'

'I would just as soon be out,' she said.

'Coping with HEs and incendiaries and fire engines and ambulances and casualties?' I asked.

'I'd sooner be on patrol on my own feet,' she said, smiling a little, 'than driving an ambulance, boxed up like that. You really cannot hear *what* is coming down.'

'That's the beauty of it,' I said. 'Keep in low gear and your thumb on the horn and there mightn't be a raid on.'

'But if you don't hear, you cannot take cover.'

'Well, you can't take cover in an ambulance,' I said.

'I don't know how you can do it,' she said. 'Now we *can* get down.'

'Sooner you than me,' I said.

'Our work is more varied,' she went on. 'That makes it much more interesting. So much detail ...'

'Forms to fill in?' I asked.

Her face lit up. Evidently she was a forms enthusiast, like Mrs Boxer. 'Most certainly. No action can be taken without written instructions. If an incident occurs, the warden must fill in an XYZ at once and send it back to the Post by messenger.'

'What on earth's an XYZ?'

She was delighted to show me the form. 'Whoever is in charge of the telephone immediately rings Report and Control and dictates this message. Accuracy is essential. Report and Control can then call out the appropriate services.'

'How do they know how many ambulances and stretcher parties to send?' I said. 'Do they just guess?'

'Certainly not. It is all worked out to a formula. So many casualties, so many stretcher parties and so many ambulances.'

'If it's fire?'

'Oh, if it's fire, you send a messenger or go yourself direct to the Fire Station. You cannot let a fire wait. But of course, you must write your message on the appropriate form.'

'And who tells the Fire Brigade what to do? You?'

She looked quite shocked. 'The Fire Services are entirely independent of us,' she explained. 'We merely report the incident and they make their own arrangements. It is for them to say where they wish to park, what hydrants they propose to use, how many pumps they will call out and whether rescue or other services can get to work. We merely co-ordinate. An incident officer takes charge at every incident.'

'Carrying blue lamps, two, one above the other,' I nodded wisely. 'I haven't seen any yet. Tell me, are there lots of women wardens. And post wardens?'

She was sure there were plenty of women wardens, and likely to be many more. She didn't see why not, either. Probably there were women post wardens, even women district wardens; she didn't see any reason, if it came to that, why there shouldn't be women incident officers. Many women were most capable organisers. But she wasn't very interested in White Hats and Blue Hats for women. Promotion didn't worry her; she was the sort of person who would take it if it came and be content if it didn't.

'I'm on the telephone to-night,' she said. 'Telephone and teas.'

I tried to tease her back to Sunday night, but she was much more interested in the problem of the tea ration, and the rumour that ARP tea was a special issue of used and salvaged tea leaves, which was why the flavour was unique. She was quite prepared to believe any infamy of government departments.

Then she switched on the electric light over her desk, and as the blurred outline of things that the dusk had hidden leapt out again, I remembered that I was due back at the Station at black-out time.

That same night, Bilson and I had a shelter call. We didn't very often have cases at shelters, for the regular ambulance service usually dealt with them, and we rather dreaded them because it was sometimes difficult to get bearers and there were generally a lot of steps to negotiate. 'It's that shelter under the chapel,' said Bilson, pondering the case sheet. 'Not a Tube ... that's something. But still,' she added gloomily, 'it's probably a baby. Hurry, Gibsy dear, we don't want her to have it in the ambulance.'

Though it was a quiet night, the heavily strutted crypt was crowded to capacity. It was warm; fans churned the thick air, sticky with the smell of damp old clothes, hot feet and sour milk, and the acrid stench of disinfectant. Every place was taken, and from the headrails of the closely ranged three-tiered bunks hung string bags and shopping bags, coats and scarves and children's frocks; brown paper parcels, holding the small treasures of a lifetime, bulged under pillows. The strident voice of the wireless was hazed with the sound of sibilant gossip, little spurts of laughter and the squealing of babies.

Nearly all the people in the top berths were in bed already, thankful to get their feet up after a hard day's work. One girl hummed a dance tune as she combed her hair and twisted it round metal curlers, and the fat woman next to her, with a pink shawl over a purple blouse, beat out the time with her spoon against her tea-cup; a cluster of children squabbled in the passage way and a group of husky toughs in oil-smeared overalls and leather jerkins leaned up a against the walls.

'I hope to goodness they don't keep us long,' said Bilson, peering anxiously round for someone in authority. She hated hanging about on a job, thinking always of other casualties who might be waiting, of work left unfinished at the Station. She lifted the corner of a blue and yellow chintz curtain which closed a recess, then let it fall as we glimpsed a row of improvised cots, bright patchwork quilts tucked round small cuddly children, and a tired mother changing a baby's nappy.

In the space between two bunks near us stood a large winged armchair, and sitting poker straight in it was a great hulk of a woman, her grey hair drawn into a top-knot and skewered with an old-fashioned spangled comb. A black shawl, fringed with white, draped her shoulders, and her worn puffy hands were clasped over a leather bag and a pale blue thermos which rested in her vast lap. Her butter-coloured face was smooth and placid, and small black eyes sparked under heavy lids.

'I sez to meself,
I says, "you don't need
to be scared till Granny is.
And I ain't never seen
'er scared yet."'

'Lookin' at Granny?' breathed a man on my right. 'She can't lie down, see? Got a illness she 'as. Sits up there night after night.'

I murmured sympathetically.

'Huh!' he snorted. 'I sez to meself sometimes, watching 'er wen things is pretty 'ot round yere, I sez to meself, I sez, "I guess you don't need to be scared till Granny is. An' I ain't never seen 'er scared yet".'

A St John nurse with a round merry face slid through the crowd and touched my arm.

'Your patient's nearly ready,' she said. 'I've got her in the sick bay. Slipped on the steps and cracked her tib and fib. We've splinted her up and she's having a cup of tea. So there's no hurry, and I'll give you a cup of tea too before you go.'

Bilson's eyes gleamed at the thought of tea; you could see she was torn between her longing to be off and the prospect of a hot drink.

'Anyway, it's not a baby,' she said, as we put down the stretcher and eased the straps of our tin hats. Somebody switched off the wireless as a man came on the platform, pushing back his dark coat, and tipping his tin hat from his head. He set it on the table, and stood there, smiling at us. Evidently he was the minister in charge of the chapel. One of the toughs shouted: 'Put up a bit of a prayer, mister.'

All the rustling movement was stilled as if a wind among trees had suddenly dropped.

'Dear God, we ask Thee to look after every one of us this night. Our Father ...'

We screwed our eyes shut and felt like children as we spoke the old comforting words.

But the silence that followed was pierced by the muted voice of the siren.

'Come along, boys and girls, give us a bit of a sing-song ...'

Feet stamped. A double line of children, small boys and little girls, big boys and pretty girls, trooped up to the platform. It was bright with the khaki and blue of Boy Scouts and Girl Guides, brilliant red kerchiefs about their necks, apple red cheeks. They scrummed round the piano. Scuffling and laughing, then suddenly intent, they swelled with pride on an indrawn breath and let it go:

'Daisy … Daisy … Give me your answer do …'

We were walled in by the roystering tune, sucked into it as into a whirlpool, the clamour of it filling our ears, the rhythm of it swinging our hearts to a steadier beat. Our voices were drawn out of us so that we sang as one person. The door against which I leant quivered as if the earth tremor from a near explosion had shaken it, but it was impossible to hear the sound of planes or the whistle of bombs, impossible even to tell if the guns were speaking. It could have been a bad raid; but all the furious noise was beaten back by that wave of song, rich and husky, silver-tipped with the children's voices.

The nurse touched my arm again.

'Come and get your tea and your casualty,' she said.

'Do these children often sing like this?' I asked as the tune changed to 'I love Sixpence … jolly little Sixpence.'

She nodded. 'So we shan't hear what's happening? Yes. Sometimes they sing all night.'

I love sixpence …

VI Christmas, 1940

We were on duty at Station X2 on Christmas Eve. The ASO had given us holly and paper streamers and there was to be a party with presents for everybody. As we came in we looked at the pile of decorations lying on the big table; then we looked quickly away and went to hang up our caps and coats.

'Christmas wouldn't be Christmas unless we decorated, would it?' said Mrs Boxer.

We went and looked at the notice board to see the driving list go up. Among the usual Service Orders which drew our attention weekly to things like not wearing forage caps instead of the official peaked ones on duty, or being on licensed premises in uniform, the servicing of vehicles and the allocation of tinned foods to canteens, was another, rather startling one, wishing us all a Happy Christmas.

We turned to the driving list. Mark and Penny were first out, and Penny was first on patrol. We did the cleaning and the odd jobs deliberately, while Mrs Boxer fidgeted with the holly and waited for us to finish. Decoration began at last.

'Gee,' said Robin, unwinding a paper streamer, 'when I was a kid, we just about filled the house with holly, my brother and I ...'

Her brother was a merchant seaman. 'Maybe he'll strike lucky and be in port this year,' she said.

Johnny fingered a silver star, then stuck it absently among her curls.

'Last year, my boy-friend was on leave ... we went to the Regalia – and did we have a good time ...'

Bilson began to sort out the holly.

'You know, when Father was alive, we always had a Christmas tree. Even when we were quite grown-up. He would have it ... D'you think I need more holly round this lamp?'

'It's fine.'

'Of course, now it's different. Since Freddy went ... well, you can't have a tree by yourself, can you? Pass up the scissors, Gibsy dear.'

Penny put her head round the door, 'I wish someone would come out and relieve me,' she said. 'I'm fed up with reading those blasted posters on the place opposite.'

We told her to go away; she'd only been out ten minutes. In another ten she was back again.

'Why don't you change those streamers round?' she said. 'So the red, white and blue come together. That'd be far better.'

We told her to go away.

We wreathed the notice board with holly and pinned a sprig of mistletoe over the Control Room door and dared the men's leader to kiss the officers.

'Why don't you get out the flag?' said Penny from the door. 'We simply must find a place for the flag.'

We ordered her out; but Johnny got the Union Jack and plastered it over the sandbags; then she fetched a bunch of chrysanthemums and pinned it slantwise across the corner.

We looked at it uncertainly. The shift-leader came and considered, hands in her pockets, head on one side, cigarette drooping from her lower lip.

'Too much like a Service funeral for my taste,' she said and walked off.

And Johnny took away the flowers, her cheeks very red.

'Ever known Christmas Eve go so slowly?' said Mark presently. 'There always used to be such a lot of shopping to do. Did you always leave everything to the last minute?'

'Always,' I said. 'I remember when Toddy was small ...'

When at last it was nearly tea-time, the long tables were pushed together, and the ASO's maid brought in quantities of cakes on great trays that covered the Control Room desks. Johnny and Penny and the ASO arranged them, and Greeny set out little red candlesticks on the tables between sprigs of holly, and Bilson followed her round, scattering crackers, her chin sticking out more obstinately than usual. Mark sat by herself near the door, where she could hear the outside phone. Her husband was on duty with his unit. She wouldn't see him, but there was a chance he might ring up.

Then people's friends and relations began to arrive, mothers and sisters, and a father or two, and some of the men's wives. It was rather fun guessing which belonged to whom.

When at last we sat down to tea we talked so loudly we had to shout to keep up with ourselves; we laughed till we choked; we ate till we felt sick; we gave each other little presents, a few cigarettes or a bar of chocolate; we pulled crackers and stuck paper caps on our heads and let off the indoor fireworks that came out of the crackers, leaning over the table, as excited as school kids to see the top hats that turned into snakes when you lit them, snatching the little sparklets and twirling them till the white sparks parodied the flares the Germans dropped.

'Look out, chaps,' said the shift-leader. 'Here's a bomb ... watch out ... she's going up.'

'Oh do be careful,' Penny said urgently. 'Do be careful – it may go bang any minute.' She cowered away like a maiden lady and put her hands over her ears, laughing as we all jumped at the minute explosion.

'If you've broken that plate,' commanded Mrs Boxer in her gruff voice, 'kindly put the pieces on my desk so that I may claim a replacement.'

Johnny got up then and went to the piano, to play for Greeny, who was musical and in great demand at amateur concerts. Greeny had changed into a long dark blue velvet frock and she gave the piano corner quite a platform air as she stood there, hands clasped round a red rose, singing old songs we all knew.

We sat round in a great semi-circle, on chairs, on benches and on tables, stamping and clapping, because after all, it was Christmas. Merry Christmas – Christmas was always merry, wasn't it?

So we stamped and clapped and laughed, and hoped that nobody there could read our secret thoughts; but I saw Johnny's mother watching her, her handkerchief rolled into a ball in her kid-gloved hand. Did she see all those other Christmases, when Johnny was a little kid, when we all believed in peace on earth and there was no terror but only kindliness and hope ... Our thoughts were like a rain of cruel arrows ...

'If only Jack's all right ...'

'If Bill's safe … perhaps they won't fly at Christmas …'

'If he'd just ring up – so I could hear his voice …'

'… they'll be toasting Absent Friends too … George, oh George …'

'… if it's tea-time here, he'll be having elevenses in Canada …'

'… When Toddy was little …'

'… the Christmas before the war …'

'… before Don was hurt …'

'… before we lost our home …'

'… before David went …'

'… before Bob was killed …'

'When we were kids …'

All the kind ghosts of every happy Christmas we had ever known were thick about us in that smoky room, sweet, sentimental happy Christmases, when children's voices shrilled about us, when we were young and simple of heart.

Greeny began to sing: 'Just a song at twilight …'

Someone switched off all the lights but the one over the piano. Greeny wasn't really so very pretty, but just then she looked quite beautiful. We blinked at her; we didn't see very well; our own dear ghosts were nearer than her face.

Then we picked up the chorus, humming and singing till the surge of traffic outside was drowned and our thoughts with them.

The lights went up, and all the friends and relations looked at their watches and began to say good-bye. We gave three cheers for the ASO. We said it had been a grand party, a terrific party, a stupendous party. The men's leader cornered the ASO under the mistletoe and kissed her while we roared our delight.

The siren went, its banshee wail cleaving across our laughter.

People hustled their friends and relations off the station as Penny and Mark hurried to the pegs and scrummed for their equipment. The first ambulance was ready for a call.

'At least *we* shan't have to wash up,' said Penny.

'Good-bye, dear. Thanks a lot. See you tomorrow.'

'Bye-bye, duckie. See you in the morning. You'll come straight home?'

'Happy Christmas ... happy Christmas ...'

Johnny's mother hung back in the doorway as gunfire crackled and the blade of a searchlight swung across the sky. Johnny put an arm round her and kissed her; one of the men went out and said it wasn't anything of a raid; it hadn't got going properly anyway, and Johnny's mother had heaps of time to get home.

'Good-bye, dearie,' said Johnny's mother. 'See you in the morning ...' And she went out.

The shift-leader said, 'For pity's sake, you girls, get a move on and clear up this mess. Can't have the place looking like a kids' party with a *raid* on.'

We got waste paper baskets and shovelled in the cracker papers and the caps and the cigarette ends and the bits of holly and the mottoes that had made us laugh.

'Maybe it's silly to try and keep Christmas,' said Robin. 'Or – maybe it's not?'

'Maybe it's not,' I said.

VII January, 1941

After Christmas it was very quiet; there were many nights with no alert at all, and Mark said the blitz was no longer what it was and sometimes she wondered if there was any point at all in sticking to the Ambulance Service.

And yet one evening, when Belinda and Penny and I were having supper just after the siren had sounded for the first time in days, we heard the familiar screech of bombs coming down. The first two whistled away, far beyond us, but the third came so close that it was like hearing an express train charging at you and wondering if you were on the main line.

I finished my bite, and still it was rushing at us, and put down my knife and fork and still it was screaming, and looked at the others and saw them wondering if it was true that when you heard a bomb it wouldn't hit you, and still the tormented air shrieked as it came. There was time to think about one's Will, about which warden's post would deal with the damage, about who was on duty at the Station to cope with our remains, to hope that one's vest hadn't a hole in it, to wish I had posted that last letter to George. The walls shook so much that you could see them quivering, and suddenly one corner of the room tipped down and a pit-prop worked loose and swung about like a pendulum.

For a moment I wondered if we had been hit, and if I was only imagining that the room was still there, with Penny and Belinda staring at me, open-mouthed, Penny with her hands over her ears waiting for the cataclysmic bang which didn't come. It seemed quite probable that we might have been killed without knowing it.

Then Belinda said, 'Perhaps it's got the Station.'

Penny said, 'Quick – oh, quick …'

We reached for our tin hats and went up the road, and at the corner, we took a deep breath and stopped. Penny shut her eyes. 'You look, Belinda,' she said. 'They're not your friends.'

'But the Station's OK,' Belinda said. 'There's a slight mess opposite, that's all.'

There certainly was a slight mess opposite. The bomb had fallen, as dramatically as if its flight had been deliberately checked, right on to the empty gutted building opposite, hurling rubble and masonry, twisted girders and a pair of iron gates into the empty road.

'Well, we won't have to read those damn' posters any more,' said Penny. 'I was sick of the sight of them anyway.'

'Thirty feet from your petrol pumps,' said Belinda in an awed voice. 'Just about thirty feet.'

'I always have believed in miracles,' said Penny. And we didn't laugh.

We went home and drank the health of the Station in Penny's emergency bottle of whisky which she kept more or less chained up in the shelter and fell asleep and were wakened by the All Clear.

In January, with the thick misty mornings, day raids surprised us by beginning again. At first, they were just tiresome because they interrupted the heavenly day-time sleep we had when we came off duty. And then one morning, Greeny, who always heard rumours first, said:

'They say that Station X4 got a direct hit. Yesterday.'

'People'll say anything,' said Robin.

'They're right for once,' said the men's leader, looming up beside us, and twisting a bit of oiled rag in his hand.

'Sure thing, X4's been hit. They caught it yesterday. I had a drink with one of their chaps. Came slap down on the canteen. Poor young Whizzer – you remember Whizzer, girls? Used to play A1 ping-pong – he's got his.'

We looked out of the one remaining window at the mess opposite. We knew X4; sometimes we played them at ping-pong; sometimes we shared a lecture with them. We all knew young Whizzer; we'd laughed because he wore his hair too long.

'Seen X4,' people would say to each other. 'No? Well, I have. It certainly shook me.'

'Heard about young Whizzer? Tough, that.'

Though raids were not very severe, we had again that queer feeling of unreality, of being surprised when we woke up in the morning and had hot coffee for breakfast.

'Going away for your next leave, Robin?' asked Mark.

'I guess I'm not making plans ahead.'

'Seeing the boy-friend next week, Johnny?'

'Maybe I will. If ...'

There was always that 'if' in the background of our lives. It made Greeny and Robin forget they'd had words over the tea-making; it sent Johnny out to scrub her ambulance without being told; it made Mrs Boxer keep us dusting gas clothing and counting blankets till we were feverish with irritation; it had Penny crouching for hours over her map, looking up hospital entrances; it kept us all together, all sharing in the dull tasks that fell to one or other of us.

At home, Penny moved the tins to a cupboard under the stairs.

'There – even if the house goes, the tins'll be absolutely safe,' she said.

'I don't see it matters much about the tins,' I said.

'But I couldn't bear anything to happen to the tins,' said Penny anxiously.

Next morning, the Alert sounded as we signed the attendance book, before the shift-leader had even got up the driving list. She told Greeny and me to stand by.

When Bilson took telephone duty and tried to call Report and Control to give our state of parties, we found the phone had packed up. The shift-leader told Bilson to nip across to the emergency phone we'd arranged to borrow in a flat across the street.

'Gibsy, you can go too, as runner,' she added. 'Take your equipment; if there's a call, you'll be ready for it.'

Guns coughed as Bilson and I went out; we could hear shrapnel tinkling against roofs and dustbins and we put on our tin hats pretty quickly. But bare-headed women were strolling down the street, carrying babies and shopping baskets. A majestic cart horse, drawing a railway van, plodded amiably along, just flicking his ears as a gun went off. Buses crowded with office workers put on an extra spurt of speed.

We dodged between them and clumped up to the flat we'd come to borrow. It belonged to a friend of the ASO's, and Bilson had the key. We flung the curtains open and switched on the electric fire and found the telephone and rang Report and Control to give the new number almost before we drew breath.

Then we pulled a couple of opulent armchairs close to the fire, put the telephone at Bilson's elbow and stretched ourselves out with our feet up.

'I'm going to enjoy this,' Bilson said. 'It's a peach of a flat.'

It was. Our cold feet were grateful for the thick carpets and the hot fire. We admired the chintzes and the lighting and peered enviously into the all-electric kitchen and the pink bathroom with its porcelain bath and shower.

'Wish I dared risk a bath,' Bilson said.

The phone rang. Report and Control were checking the line. Bilson found a pile of magazines.

The phone rang. Report and Control reported a hospital as full.

'Getting busy,' said Bilson, pushing away the magazines.

The phone rang. A thin voice said, 'This is Everyman's Stores speaking. We so much regret we cannot supply any more pink lavatory paper. Would madam care for green?'

The phone rang. 'One ambulance, one car...' said Report and Control.

I picked up the message as Bilson scribbled it out and pelted down into the street; it was still thick with traffic, the pavements blocked with morning shoppers.

'First ambulance, first car,' I squeaked breathlessly as I reached the Control Room. Penny jumped up to take my place as runner; Greeny grabbed her First Aid kit, the shift-leader took down particulars, and we were out before the ASO had time to say Hurry.

All the ordinary traffic was still snarling along the road, and at the crossing where the lights had jammed, the policeman on point duty would not give us the right of way though I kept my thumb on the horn. We crept along behind a lorry, were baulked by a laundry van, bullied a Rolls Royce into the gutter and shot ahead. Greeny gave a squeak; she hated to be driven fast. The road was greasy and it was tricky work, cornering with that top-heavy box body.

The incident had happened just behind a railway station, We didn't need to look for it, because of the crowd of people surging across the road: typists on a lunch hour stroll, middle-aged women up from the suburbs, business men who thought perhaps they could give a hand, and errand boys wanting a thrill. They pushed and jostled, and pressed forward, eyes bulging, mouths gaping, greedy for second-hand horror.

'Beasts,' said Greeny viciously. 'Getting in the way just so they can go home with a good bomb story to-night … *Beasts.*'

A woman warden came across the road to us. Her grey hair was crisply curled, her face had the porcelain look of good make-up. Between her tin hat and her top boots she was so elegant she might have been lunching in a smart restaurant.

Greedy for second-hand horror …

'Turn and back down here, will you?' she said. 'Your casualty's waiting.'

'Can you get the people away?' said Greeny, scrambling out to see me back.

'Clear the road there!' There was an edge to the woman's voice. 'What do you think this is? A football match? Clear the road or I'll fetch over the police.'

Sheepish, almost apologetic, they gave ground, only to press forward as I passed them.

I backed slowly to Greeny's careful signals, hearing a familiar crackle under my wheels as I pulled up by a side turning so blue with glass that it shone like a tiny glacier in the faint winter sun.

A bomb had carried away the parapet of one building and penetrated the basement of another. In the road was a crumpled car, like a toy a child had trodden on. You couldn't see if there had been any one inside.

Mayfair warden.

The stretcher party came out, carrying an elderly woman with a bandage round her head. Her noisy breathing sounded above the drone of the engine. Greeny got in beside her, tucked the blanket round and took her limp hands in her own.

Through the open hatch I could hear her voice.

'You'll be all right, Mother. You're safe now. You'll be quite all right. I promise you you'll be all right.'

Perhaps she couldn't hear or feel or see – but if she did, then Greeny's voice must have sounded good to her just then.

As I slid the gear in, a thin, middle-aged woman in a short fur coat, with a scarf round her head, ran out of the house, stumbling over the rubble on the steps, to clutch at the warden's sleeve.

'You can't leave me behind. I'm her sister. You can't leave me behind.'

The warden looked at me and I looked at the warden.

'Can you take her in front – or is it against the regulations?'

'Blow the regulations.'

So she came in front: I drove slowly for the back tyre was soft; probably the glass had done for it. And all the time, as I threaded my way through the nonchalant civilian traffic, that little woman talked. She and her sister had only come up from the country that day, because they didn't want to leave their little home too long … 'and staying with relations, well, it's awkward sometimes, isn't it? It seemed quite all right to come up … everybody said the worst was over … and when things are quiet, people in the country aren't quite so glad to have you, are they? So we came back …'

Minnie's sister.

Very carefully, I negotiated the roundabout; a taxi cut across in front of me so that I had to brake and check a skid … the back tyre was definitely soft.

'… I said to my sister, Minnie, if the warning's gone, we ought to go to the shelter. Really we ought. But she said no one went to shelter in the day-time now. I said we ought to go to the shelter … I had a queer feeling … when something's going to happen I always *know* … But Minnie wouldn't listen. I said Minnie, you ought not to sit by the window. Not by the window, I said … with all that glass. And not even sticky paper on it. I said Minnie, to please me come away from the window …

And then it happened … it was like being smothered in glass … '

I shot a look at her; one of her hands was roughly bandaged, and there was a red streak showing through.

'Is your hand bleeding still?' I said, wondering if I ought to stop the car and see to it.

She looked at it as though it wasn't hers and said it was all right.

'You ought to have it in a sling. Keep it *up*.'

But she didn't listen. 'I kept calling Minnie … it wasn't like Minnie to give way …'

'I'll take you to the First Aid Post and get that hand dressed,' I said.

She stopped talking and began to laugh; laughter gurgled in her throat and sprayed out wildly.

'Stop that,' I said roughly.

She was quiet at once. We turned into the hospital gates and she said, 'The ceiling's down, all over the beds. Minnie will be so cross. Oh dear, oh dear, Minnie *will* be cross.'

I got out and opened the door for her.

She clutched hold of me. 'Don't leave me,' she said.

Greeny and the stretcher bearers coped with Minnie, and I took my patient to the First Aid Post in the far wing of the hospital, across a garden where the first bulbs were springing through the grass already.

I took Minnie's sister to the desk at the entrance to the long white-tiled room, with its treatment tables in the centre, and its steriliser hissing in a corner, where a clerk in a white overall was entering particulars of each case. Together we coaxed her name and address from her; the clerk wrote them on a label and tied it to Minnie's wrist.

'Then we needn't worry you with questions any more,' she said.

I waited till a pretty child in a Red Cross uniform had taken charge of Minnie's sister, got her into a chair, produced a cup of tea, spoken to the Sister with the St John Cross on her cap, and begun to peel the bandage very gently from Minnie's sister's hand. She looked about nineteen, and her movements were light and free, as if, perhaps, she'd been a dancer. The steriliser hissed and bubbled, steam clouding the air, as another girl whipped out bowls and kidney dishes with a pair of Cheatle's forceps. Another girl wheeled a small trolley, complete with kidney dishes, forceps, iodine, scissors, gut, needles in methylated spirit, up to a man whose head was being shaved by a youngster who held her bottom lip between her teeth, crimson with concentration. They tucked a towel round his head, and the youngster put her hands on his shoulders to steady him while the St John Sister put a couple of stitches in the cut. You could see her wince in sympathy and look away as the needle prodded through the flesh. Probably it was her first real casualty, and though she'd often prepared a stitch trolley in practices, this was the first time she'd seen it used.

'There – there's nothing to it, you see,' said Sister briskly.

I heard Minnie's sister check a little moan as the bandage came off.

'You'll look after her now?' I said to the clerk. 'Her sister's pretty bad, and she's shot to bits.'

'Of course we will. It's hard on the older ones, isn't it?'

'She's got nowhere to go to-night,' I said.

'That's all right. We'll pack her off to a Rest Centre if she's fit.'

I nodded. I wanted to wait and see what happened. But Minnie's sister was all right. One kind voice was like another to her.

Greeny was waiting when I got back.

'The off tyre's soft,' she said.

'It'll see us through,' I said as I kicked it. 'Do we report back?'

Greeny nodded. 'Yes … there may be some trapped casualties in that basement.' She turned up the collar of her coat. 'Chilly, isn't it? Jerry's still overhead.'

'He certainly is … funny, I never noticed till now …'

'You'd think half the people in the streets didn't know there was a raid on … if it were dark they'd be in their shelters, listening to the guns …'

'I suppose it never seems so bad by day, when you can see?'

'Unless you see too much … Goodness – *that* was a bomb …'

When we got back to the incident, it had grown bigger. The bomb that Greeny heard had landed at the far end of the street, bringing the corner of a house down, hurling its fragments into the road among the crowds.

The same warden hurried over to us. Her smart coat was muddied, brick dust filmed her make-up, her hat was white with plaster: 'Can you two go and give the stretcher parties a hand? That last bomb's made a good few casualties …'

Greeny was sprinting down the road, glass crackling under her feet, first aid kit bumping against her side. I took out the ignition key and followed – with some blankets. Dotted up and down the road, little groups of men and women knelt by people who were hurt. The white hats of wardens and stretcher party leaders looked like mushrooms.

On the pavement, a girl, fair-haired, red-lipped, lay by herself, quite still and quiet, with no one by her. I turned to go to her, but the Mayfair warden moved more quickly, looked down, and dropped a ground-sheet over her. She didn't need any one's help.

I stumbled on, and almost tripped over a great block of masonry, and my foot kicked away a boot that lay there by itself. I stooped to pick it up … it was a small brown boot, quite new and shiny. Somebody might be looking for it. It was a good boot. I carried it quite a way before I realised it had a foot inside. As I dropped it, I sicked into the gutter.

'Hurry, Gibsy,' called Greeny.

She was kneeling by a youngish man, who lay on his face.

'Put the blanket down, so we turn him on to it … Ready? Roll him over …'

As we turned him back on to the blanket, and his head came towards us, his features were so masked in blood, he didn't seem to have a face.

'Cotton wool … a couple of dressings … roller bandage … three tri's.' I fumbled in the First Aid kit … when I looked at him again, Greeny said, 'He's all right – cut over the eye … broken nose and half a dozen teeth out … concussed …'

I forced myself to watch; I forgot about feeling sick. By the time we'd bandaged him, he opened his eyes and we swabbed up the blood that trickled back from his lids and down the fan of creases and into the ruts about his neck.

A couple of wardens gave us a hand, and we got him on to a stretcher, four of us carrying him through the rubble and the glass. As the stretcher clanged in to the runners two more bearers came up with another.

'Priority case … haemorrhage … got a tourniquet on …'

'Look sharp,' said Greeny to me. 'Get off at once, will you?'

Taxis and private cars were still humming up the main road; buses packed with shoppers trundled along; cyclists pedalled homewards, and a van from Everyman's Stores passed us on a corner. Perhaps it had been delivering Madam's green lavatory paper.

When we'd finished at the hospital, Greeny came in front with me.

As we drove into our own yard, she said: 'I *hate* these daylight raids. You *see* too damn' much.'

VIII January, 1941

As we came off duty next day, Greeny said: 'I keep thinking of that fellow we picked up ...'

'I keep wondering about Minnie's sister,' I said.

'We might go along to hospital and find out,' said Greeny.

'We might.' I wondered if Greeny felt as tired as I did; she'd put the make-up on so lavishly that it was hard to tell.

'We shan't sleep for ages if we *do* go home,' said Greeny, checking a yawn. 'Come on.'

It had rained all night, and the air was washed clean of the fumes of high explosive and charred wood. Ordinary life had closed defiantly over the drama of yesterday. Only at the corner, by the bombed flats, rescue parties still worked, seeking to free the trapped casualties, and an ambulance from another section stood optimistically waiting.

At the top of the road we parted, for we had taken Greeny's casualties to one hospital and Minnie to another; besides, I should have to spend time tracing her through the First Aid Post people. So I went up the cinder path to the Post. The night shift was coming off duty when I arrived; some wore street clothes because they were going to offices; they did not look very tired; but the girls who were going home to sleep had not bothered to wash and re-do their faces, and they had that curious, strained, grey look that morning brings to people who have only slept an hour or two on a stretcher or in a chair.

'Bye-bye, see you Monday ...'

'Hope the boss is in a good temper,' laughed one. 'I feel I can't read my own shorthand at the moment.'

When I went in, I found a different group on duty. The clerk who was checking over records wasn't even the same, and none of the nurses had been there when I took Minnie's sister. Indeed, the whole place looked different; it wasn't just that all the tables were bare because they were being swabbed over, or that the girls were rolling bandages and padding splints and chattering; somehow it was quite impossible to imagine that yesterday the room had been crowded with living people who were hurt, when to-day it looked exactly as if it were being put ready for an examination in First Aid.

'There will be a bandaging practice at eleven,' said the Sister-in-charge.

'*Another* practice,' said one little nurse, pouting as she flicked a duster along the shelf. 'I *wish* I'd been on duty yesterday. I'm *never* on when there's a raid ... That's the worst of being a secretary four days a week ... who cares if the man's beastly letters get answered or not? It's *futile*.'

'You'll get your turn, don't you worry,' said Sister. 'And a lot of use you'll be if you can't even dust a shelf. Take these bottles down and do it properly.'

The tough, middle-aged records clerk smiled to herself, and, as she asked me what I wanted, she explained under her breath that they kept a skeleton staff of fully trained nurses, one to each shift, and that all the rest were volunteers, some trained by the Red Cross, some by St John Ambulance Brigade. This was a post run by the Borough ARP authorities, not like others which were administered directly by a Red Cross Detachment. But the work they did was the same, and the people who helped were nearly all unpaid. Mostly the ones who came by day hadn't their living to earn; some of them were still at home with their families, and some were older and their families had already gone and left them behind. And mostly the ones who worked by night were girls with jobs in the City or behind counters during the day.

'There's ever such a lot of feeling, too,' she said, 'between the ones who've had to treat real casualties and the ones who haven't. Funny, too, how the same shift always seem to come in for the trouble. Just a minute, dear, and I'll look up your case ... yes ... here she is ...'

Minnie's sister had had a couple of stitches in her hand and been treated for shock and then passed on to the Rest Centre.

'The one at St Bridget's School. Know it?'

I did.

'You'll find her there. They're bound to keep her to-day.'

St Bridget's School stood in the middle of a festering cluster of mean streets, long overdue for slum clearance, the sort of spot where men and women can shiver and be hungry within sight of luxury flats where other men and women dine at ease. It was an old, grey, uninviting building; the drab bricks looked tired, as if they were weary of listening to multiplication tables. In the asphalt yard, where the girls had played netball, there were bins of sand and buckets of water, and broad, white painted arrows that guided you to a door marked Infants. You pushed through thick curtains into a narrow space between more curtains, and a musty depression gripped you, as if hundreds of other people had paused on the threshold and thought miserably: 'Well, it's come to this. Everything's gone.'

But inside, you cheered up at once. The big hall was rather like a gaudy tea-room at a seaside resort, the kind where they paint sunshine on the walls to encourage you if it's raining outside. Bright wicker armchairs stood about, the bunks were covered with cheerful check dust-sheets, and someone had painted the walls themselves with brilliant country scenes. There was a hayfield, with a wagon and stout white horses, a river, garnished with improbable buttercups, and a wood, unnaturally blue with bluebells. Large painted birds were nesting in trees garlanded with strange flowers.

I blinked at them, and a woman in a green WVS overall fussed up cheerfully, with a cup of tea on a tray.

'Did the wardens send you, dear?' she asked.

I said, 'No-o,' and she said, 'Now be a good girl and drink up your tea before we take particulars.'

I said hastily that I wasn't a case, and she said Oh dear, I mustn't have the tea if I hadn't been bombed out, and if I was just making inquiries I'd better see the Welfare Adviser.

'I just want to trace someone,' I said.

'The Welfare Adviser will help you. Ask her anything you like – she knows all the answers.'

So I went up to a table in the corner, and waited while the Welfare Adviser disposed of a voluble lady who had lost all her money when her handbag was blown up with her house. She

Welfare Adviser.

looked surprisingly young for the job; her fair, untidy hair was tied back with a brown ribbon, and she wore a salmon pink jumper and a pepper and salt tweed skirt. She beckoned me over to the chair by her side. What was my name? What did I want? What, if anything, had I lost?

Her voice had the note one hears in the voices of really good children's nannies, the note that says it is just no use making a fuss. I asked about Minnie's sister and added, out of deference to the voice, that I didn't want to worry her if she were busy.

She wasn't busy; she had been busy: she would be busy, but just now she was quite prepared to discuss Minnie's sister, and she placed her at once.

'Difficult type,' she said. 'No self-reliance.'

I said perhaps one wouldn't have much after being bombed.

'But most of them are very good. Only, of course, *she's* had a comfortable life. It's a handicap when it comes to trouble. Most of them are poor. *My* problem is they will never leave their own neighbourhoods if they can help it. You can offer them billets in the country or flats in Mayfair, and they turn up their noses.'

'You'd think they'd be thankful to go somewhere quiet.'

'Quiet? They hate quiet. Besides they don't want to leave their friends. Nor would you – if you had their friends. They never think twice about taking in half a dozen extra – or sharing their kitchens or their coppers or their beds ...'

It was her job to act as sheep-dog to the homeless, to see that they were put in touch with the proper authority for rehousing, for compensation, for convalescence, for evacuation, for new clothes. She saw that their cases were dealt with at once, that they weren't bullied into taking decisions they didn't want to take, that they didn't leave her care till they were fit to fend for themselves. She was a living blue-book; she knew exactly what authority – and what committee of what authority – dealt with every problem, and what charitable organisation could be called in to help. There was a man in charge of the Rest Centre, but you felt that this girl's personality gave the place its vitality and its efficient kindliness, and you knew that she was prepared to wrestle with rules and regulations and red tape like a strong man with a bar of iron, till their rigidity bent to meet the needs of each individual.

'Did those people come in yesterday?' I asked, looking away from her towards a little group, sitting by the fire at the far end of the room, two elderly men and three women, the women nursing brown paper parcels on their laps as if they could not bear to let them out of their sight. A couple of small children in knitted pixie suits of blue and pink came slithering and sliding down the room with a small harassed mother sh-shushing at their heels.

'All except the twins. They've been here a week; waiting to be evacuated; she's changed her mind twice.'

'There are darts and billiards and a writing-room upstairs,' the Welfare Adviser went on, 'but sometimes I think it takes them all their time just to sit quiet. Often I wonder if we really understand what goes on in their minds. They have the most curious little worries; they agitate about a cat or an insurance card or a best hat … you think it's silly, till you see the big worry underneath.'

'I suppose they mostly come from that nasty little street where the last bomb fell yesterday,' I said. 'A good thing that place has gone …'

'Well – I don't know. At first, when I looked at the little houses behind here, all in bits and pieces, I used to say: Another slum gone. Good riddance. But it's a good many homes gone too. It isn't all that easy to put homes together again – even if all the people are there … and often they aren't.'

I asked if they had an awful job with the people when they first came in; she shook her head. Nearly always they were very quiet. 'We have to treat for shock, of course. Hot tea and biscuits immediately – that's our rule. I remember one old man who wouldn't drink his – we thought he was being obstinate. Then we found he wanted a gargle – his mouth was so full of plaster he couldn't swallow.'

We'd drifted away from Minnie's sister, but the Welfare Adviser called up the trained nurse, and asked her to take me to the quiet room.

Nurse was a nice chatty little dumpling; she was quite glad to have a visitor, because the Centre wasn't very busy now raids were slackening off. 'We've plenty of time to make improvements,' she said. 'I like having a job where you can make improvements. This was a regular old barn when we came first – and look at it now. Gives you something to do, too, when nothing happens. Twenty-four hours on duty and twenty-four hours off, we work. And twenty-four hours with nothing happening seems ever so long.'

'You're telling me,' I said.

The quiet room had been a cloakroom before, but pegs and boot racks had gone, and there were proper beds with green coverlets, and a crib as well.

'If they're badly shocked – or a wee bit troublesome, we put them here,' she said. 'It doesn't do to let them sit with the others if they're upset.'

So Minnie's sister lay in the end bed, wearing a pink flannel wrapper, and fingering a pretty little bag which held a comb and safety pins and oddments and pencil and writing paper. American women had sent them over, Nurse said, so that English women should have the little things no woman could be happy without.

As we came in, a stout old party with a fringe sat up in bed and beckoned to me.

'Don't you think there's anything the matter with me, dearie,' she mumbled. 'Cause there ain't. On'y I lost me new teeth, see? And I'm not easy in company without me teeth.'

I asked Minnie's sister if there was anything she wanted, or any one I could write to for her, but she was still worrying about the bedroom ceiling.

'I can't quite remember how much came down,' she said. 'If it isn't too bad, I could go home, couldn't I? I'd sooner go home. I daresay Minnie would like me to go home; I ought to keep an eye on things ... the suitcases, I can't think quite where we put the suitcases, but Minnie wouldn't like it if they got lost ...'

I said I'd find out just how Minnie was, but as I went out, Nurse said she was in touch with the hospital and Minnie wasn't too well. I could go across myself if I liked; she'd be pleased to have the latest news.

Outside in the lounge, the little group was still sitting round the fire. One of the women organisers brought them tea; they thanked her and smiled, but the tea grew cold before they could bring themselves to drink it.

As we passed, Nurse said, 'Well, Grannie, and how are we feeling now?' They all looked up and spoke.

'Mustn't grumble ...'

'Me and the missus are pretty well, thank'ee.'

'We're the lucky ones.'

You could see that they were remembering friends who hadn't been so lucky, chaps who would never buy a pint in a pub again, kids who'd never racket along the roads on roller skates, women who'd never jostle around the barrows for bargains. They just sat and remembered and waited, and slowly braced themselves to face a new beginning among unfamiliar faces.

'Like to see the other sleeping rooms?' asked Nurse in my ear. 'The family room – we like to keep families together when we can … we don't want to make it like an institution – they hate that … the washrooms, the kiddies' playroom – one of the lady workers gave all the furniture, from her own nurseries, you know, when she sent her children away – the kitchens, yes, we have our own. We used to have meals sent in by caterers, but it didn't always work well after a rough night. So we supply them here …'

She showed me round, proud that I thought everything so nice, was surprised to find it so bright.

'Don't you like our pictures? Such a clever girl did them; she's on the other shift … used to do show cards and fashions … we all got together and bought the paint … couldn't have the place look dingy, could we?'

'It's a lucky thing that bomb was no nearer you,' I said.

She nodded: 'So trying when you have to move out just as you've got things to rights. I was at another Centre in the autumn; we'd just got nicely settled when we had to turn out for a time bomb in the middle of the night. Quite a business, waking everybody up and getting them out. I felt so sorry for the poor dears – some had only just come in … we had to walk ever so far too. … the roads were blocked … they were so good … I remember one girl on crutches … she'd just come to us from another school … her third move that night … she started singing that old song, you know, "Felix Keeps on Walking" … You had to laugh.'

As I left, I saw a fat bushy-faced man go up to the Welfare Adviser's table and pound it with a grimy fist.

'I reckon no one can't keep us out of our 'ome,' he said. 'Wot if there is a 'ole in the roof an' no water? Me and my old 'ooman'd sooner sleep in our own 'ome than in any ruddy 'otel.'

The heavy curtains muffled his voice as I went out and on to the hospital, noticing for the first time the desolation in which it stood. Somehow, whenever I'd gone there in a raid, I'd never noticed anything but its square silhouette, comfortingly substantial; it had always seemed such a haven; you felt you'd reached sanctuary at last when you came to its doors. Now I saw how one wing was crumpled, how fire had blackened its walls, how blast had shattered its windows. The operating theatres were in the basement these days, the upper floors were closed. I went through the big main hall which had always been so full of bustle; as I was in uniform the porter let me go up to Minnie's ward, so I could have a word with Sister.

It was a new, bright ward, less sunny than it used to be, because so much of the glass had gone, more crowded, too, because extra beds had been set up. Routine, the familiar, nerve-saving routine, slid along as usual; a young house surgeon was finishing a round, a couple of probationers were taking in hot drinks. It was hard to guess, even from their pale faces, shadowed with fatigue, that their nights were broken, their days doubly arduous, shadowed always by the responsibility of caring for the sick in danger. One day, I thought, somebody who knew and loved the hospitals would write the story of their doctors and nurses in the blitz. It would be worth reading.

Sister was sympathetic; her patients weren't just case sheets, and she clucked with concern over Minnie and Minnie's sister, who couldn't fend for themselves.

As I turned to go there was a sudden stir of interest; people sat forward and looked towards the door, and a youngish woman in a brilliant red apron brought in a trolley load of books. It was awkward, turning the corner by the screens which had been put round an emergency bed, and as I gave a hand with the trolley, I said: 'D'you mean to tell me this hospital still runs to a library?'

The book girl blinked at me through horn rims.

'Definitely. Not just this one, either. We're the International Guild of Hospital Libraries – we supply most of the London hospitals and lots of the provincial ones.'

'Even in the blitz?'

'But specially in the blitz. It's harder to be ill and have to lie and think in these days, isn't it? Books do help – specially the right books.'

I asked if I could see how it worked … I could, most certainly. They needed helpers … so many people had full-time jobs now … two days a week and half a dozen helpers at least, it took, to cover all the wards working here.

'Well now, I'm really glad to see you,' said Sister as she passed. 'Several new patients … casualties … so do get them to read. It'll take their minds off.'

'Nothin' like a love story to make you ferget that old sirene,' said a perky little woman, with her arm in plaster, reaching her good hand towards the trolley.

'Now I wonder what you'd like?' said the book girl earnestly. 'I've brought some fascinating travel books … they make such a change … how about trying something really *interesting*?'

'That's right … really interesting … a nice love story, dear …'

The book girl gave her E M Dell and moved on, checking a little sigh.

'One does like to help them to read,' she said. 'Books on China or Russia, or India … they're so topical. They make you think. But it's almost a waste of time to put them on the trolley. Still, I do get a few readers …

She brightened as a girl asked for *The Good Earth*.

'Such a fine book … you'll enjoy that … it really is good reading …'

'I dunno about that. But I guess it must be all right if they made a film of it.'

Suddenly there was a crackle of gunfire, the stutter of machine-gunning and a most unpleasant bang. I checked a start – but nobody else needed to, except one large lady who said 'Oooh,' and clapped her hand over her mouth. 'Oh Lor', I can't think what made me do that,' she said with a giggle. 'Come on, dear, let me have a look at them books.'

When we left the ward, it was quiet except for the soft flutter of turning pages. The book girl smiled: 'It's nice to see them reading, isn't it?'

She went pattering down the corridor because she had a men's ward to do before lunch. 'And I must dress the trolley again … you see the men like *good* stuff.'

The library had the quiet that many books always bring when people love them and care for them. Five thousand books there were; that meant a lot of cataloguing and card-indexing and behind-the-scenes work keeping records. I watched the book girl dress the trolley. Out came the love stories and the society memoirs, on went detective and wild west and Damon Runyon and tough travel and history and science. The book girl's face glowed with pleasure; she'd been able to get her men to read.

'We've been in luck here,' said the book girl as we went down to the men's ward. 'The lift's never been out of action. But at one of the hospitals, the only lift they can use has been busted up by a time bomb, and they have to carry the books up and down in baskets.'

The ward was a happy, pleasant place, walls a warm cream, blue and white check curtains to each bed, blue rubberised flooring that deadened the heaviest footfall.

A boy in the nearest bed sat up and waved.

'Got any murders with plenty of blood?' he said. 'I like a bit of excitement, see?'

We swung the trolley round and he drummed his fingers along the spines.

'This one has three corpses to my certain knowledge,' I said.

'That's the stuff.'

'Why not try travel for a change?' begged the book girl.

'I guess I've done enough travelling,' he said. 'I'd sooner have a bit of excitement.'

He was a merchant seaman; he'd been torpedoed twice.

The next patient looked so ill that it seemed kinder to pass him by. But the book girl went and stood quietly at the foot of his bed, and he opened his eyes as though he'd felt her smile.

'Got that book on Spain?' he whispered. 'I don't feel so good to-day, but maybe tomorrow …'

She looked out the story he wanted and put it into his locker and smiled at him again. 'You'll enjoy it tomorrow,' she said confidently, and we went away, to an elderly man, propped up on his pillows, blowing asthmatically through a walrus moustache, eyes wandering restlessly round, fingers pulling at the sheet, a lump of inert, hopeless boredom.

'How about a book for you?'

'I dunno as I can bother.'

'Something to make you *think* a bit – that'll pass the time?'

He hesitated. 'Got anything about 'orses? Racing and such?' he said at last.

We had; we'd a couple of old Nat Goulds tucked away among the trash. I got them out and he fingered them. Then he pushed them away peevishly, only to pull one back, peering at us suspiciously.

'Ow much?'

'Nothing at all. It's free. Have both – half a dozen if you like.'

His heavy face lightened – but you couldn't tell whether it was the prospect of having something to read, or the chance of getting something for nothing in a world where you got damn' all for fourpence.

Down by the fire, we found a group of regular readers now convalescing. They pushed back their chairs and came over to inspect.

'Got something about 'istory? Wiv a bit of spice in it?'

'Were you able to get me that tome on astronomy I wanted? Oh, that's fine … that'll do me for a week.'

'Got something to raise a laugh?'

'Ave you a real good book, lass,' said a grumpy little Lancashire man, 'somethin' with meat in it?'

We said we had plenty.

'Not this modern stuff. Somethin' solid. 'Ow about 'Obbs' *Leviathan*?'

We promised to find him a copy.

'Not that he'll read it,' said the book girl as we went on. 'He spends his time thinking up unlikely books and asking for them. It's provoking. Now we'll check the returns – bother, I seem to be about a dozen books short.'

'On the table in the ante-room, my dear,' said Sister briskly as she passed. 'Your pal in number seven spent most of yesterday hunting them up for you.'

We tracked down the books, and the book girl explained how when you gave out a book, you took away the card that lived in the pocket inside the back cover and tucked it into a special envelope that stayed on the trolley when you'd entered the name and bed number. Then, when you'd got all your books returned, you matched the cards to the books and saw at once if there were any missing. It was an almost foolproof system.

'Has to be,' she said. 'We get a lot of people who can only do a day now and then. People like yourself – with other jobs to do.'

Then there was all the business of keeping books in order: there were depots, she told me, where people – older people who wanted a sitting job – learned to re-sew tattered copies and to bind Penguins in gay wallpapers. Some of them worked specially for military hospitals, collecting, repairing, rebinding, a thousand books a month. They'd worked unperturbed in all the daylight raids, too busy with their glue-pots and their presses to notice if there were an Alert.

We wheeled the trolley back more slowly than we'd come. It seemed much heavier. If you weren't very young, or had another full-time job, you'd get pretty tired, pushing that trolley around; when you'd done, you'd have records to make out, books to put away, half a dozen humdrum unexciting jobs. And as I looked at the book girl's face, I thought what a lot of hope and kindness she'd spent, just helping people to choose books, when perhaps, with bad news and worries of her own, hope, kindness, confidence weren't too easy to come by.

'Come again,' she said as I said good-bye. 'Do. I know you people work awfully hard and do canteens and things in your time off. But it's just as important to give people books as it is to give them cups of tea. Really it is.'

When I went out, the guns were still firing; a thin, brave line of snowdrops showed dazzling against the blackened earth in the garden, and somewhere, among the grimy trees, a bird was singing its heart out – as if the pandemonium were no more than a thunderstorm heralding fine weather. Its treble made a line of light against the dark noise of the guns.

IX February, 1941

It was viciously cold; even the blast wall and the shutters and the black-out curtains could not muffle the draught that iced the back of my neck. In the next bunk, Penny was still snoring gently, but Belinda was up and at the telephone. Her light voice drifted down the basement stairs.

'Shorthanded? Too bad ... Yes ... definitely ... Of course I could ... No ... no ... she'd *love* to come ... I won't bother to ask her ... I know she would ... I'll bring her along at nine.'

I heard the ping of the receiver going back to rest, and Belinda came pattering down, the heels of her mules clicking against the stairs. I put my head under the bedclothes, for Belinda's voice had rippled with mischief. She was certainly up to something and I didn't want to be entangled. After all, Penny was a sort of aunt of Belinda's and it was only fair that she should be teased first.

But Belinda didn't even try to wake Penny; she just tweaked the blanket off my shoulders and the draught whistled down my backbone.

'I know perfectly well you're awake, Mildred. And you would love to come, wouldn't you?'

'I'm not and I wouldn't,' I said, clutching at the avalanche of blankets which was sliding from my upper bunk. But once the blankets from an upper bunk slip, you're done: you can't grab them back but must pursue them to the floor, and by the time your feet have gone numb on the lino, you might as well stay out of bed and get credit for being an early riser.

'But you *said* you'd love it,' said Belinda. Her brown hair was standing up in a little hedge of curls, she had a red and yellow check coat clasped round her, and the legs of her husband's blue flannel pyjamas concertinaed over her toes.

'You said,' she went on with the candid reproachfulness of a child which has caught a grown-up trying to evade a promise, 'You said you'd simply love to come and do a day on my tea-cars, any time. You asked me to fix it and now I have. Because they're short-handed and you'd really be a help.'

'Try Penny.'

'Penny wouldn't do at all; she's the wrong shape. And you're out of bed now so you might just as well come.'

I wound a blanket round my shoulders and went up to the bathroom with dignity.

When I pulled up the curtains the street looked as if it had been wrapped in cotton wool, and the grey sky seemed to droop over it, heavy with more snow. I didn't wonder so many of Belinda's canteen ladies had chills: any one, I thought crossly, would have severe and expensive chills if they drove draughty little tea-cars through blizzards. I got out a pair of George's long woollen pants, and there was a hole in the knee; so I got out the other pair, and it had a hole in the seat. I put on the first pair; I put on two vests and found a safety pin for the broken shoulder straps, and pulled two jumpers over my flannel shirt, and then I found I couldn't raise my arms to do my hair.

By the time that Belinda called out that breakfast was ready, I was cherishing a grievance. When you virtuously do something you don't want to do and know that you are being put on and know that everyone else knows you are being put on and admires you, you can enjoy it. But when you are doing something you ought to want to do and don't, when you can't even enjoy not wanting to do it and haven't any sympathy for yourself, that sort of grievance spoils your breakfast. The tea wasn't really cold and the porridge wasn't really lumpy and Belinda wasn't really a casual young woman who made use of one; but my boots pinched my chilblains and my pants were too tight and my neck was stiff and my throat tickled and I felt too old and tired for this war or for the peace that would follow it. Like Lot's wife, I just wanted to give up and go back to what I'd been used to. Half-way through breakfast, I wondered how many other middle-aged women preparing to go to offices or canteens or hospitals or WVS centres felt the same now and again. Quite a few, maybe. All the ones who'd had comfortable lives.

Mrs Dove was washing the steps as we went out; she had been up by six; she did our house and canteen work every day and wasn't off her feet till bed-time. It occurred to me that Mrs Dove was sixty if a day. And Miss Pym, my woman warden, who did three nights a week after teaching book-keeping, she was well over fifty. They hadn't had easy lives. Oh well, one would just have to get over having been pampered. That was all.

Belinda was wearing a neat grey uniform: it wasn't quite so pretty as the bus conductors', not as stylish as the tailored Sherwood green of the WVS. But it was a lot better than ours. Only, of course, it was by no means free.

'It's not compulsory,' said Belinda. 'We've quite a lot of people who don't wear uniforms and yet they're very good workers. But I think you feel happier in uniform these days – and it does save one's clothes.'

She went kicking through the snow like a schoolgirl. The air felt as if it had been washed. It was all so soft and white that you could almost imagine that man had been handed a clean sheet of paper on which he could start again to draw what he liked. But by the time we got to the main road, the old familiar silhouette of smutty chimneys, mean houses and blackened ruins was working through, like the lines of a bad drawing that would not rub out after all.

We got down to the headquarters of Belinda's Mobile Canteens at ten to nine. They had taken over a famous restaurant, and we went in at the old staff entrance, into a dim, tiled room which was once the kitchen. Part of it was fitted with enormous racks and very big tables; part of it still had sinks and stoves. There was a cloud of steam in that part and a babble of women in the other.

The passageway from the door was narrow and we got wedged in a crowd of people carrying jugs and buckets and cash boxes and stores, calling to each other to hurry up, darling, and get the van and see to the urns.

'Blast,' said Belinda. 'We're five minutes late. We shan't get a decent van and what's the betting the best cakes have gone?'

They hadn't; a man whistled to us to move on, and there were the cake trays, masses of them, just coming in from the vans of the wholesalers. The trays slid on to the racks so that one side of the room was walled with cake, like the witch's gingerbread cottage.

I wedged myself between two sets of shelves on which enamel jugs were ranged while Belinda elbowed her way to the notice-board and read out the order of the day. Each van had a definite round for the morning and another for the afternoon, and the name of the driver and attendant was written against each. Belinda and I were together.

'We'll need three urns at least, we've got a gun-site,' said Belinda. 'They only do about 150 cups each. I'll see about that if you'll scrum round and bag a couple of enamel jugs and fill them with hot water. Don't go above the red line or they'll only splash over on the way.'

I turned round and snatched two jugs and bore them triumphantly to the sink and people milled behind me and said Damn it, who had taken all the jugs and why on earth couldn't there be more jugs and how could they go out without a jug to take the hot water for washing up.

When I went out to the vans I met a wind fit to slice my ears off. Other people before me had spilled water on the steps and slopped milk from the great cans that stood in the porch. I just skidded where the spills had been and added another six inches to the toboggan slide.

I slithered and spilled.

Belinda popped her head out of a neat khaki van and backed it capably to the kerb, scrunching over frozen snow.

'It'll be tricky driving to-day,' she said. 'But you bet the boys will be glad to see us. Accelerate a bit, can you? Got the jugs?'

I picked them up, slithered and spilled. Belinda just laughed. 'We don't need to do much washing up on this round,' she said. 'In you get.'

As I helped her to undo the catch of the door, my damp fingers almost stuck to the cold metal. Inside, there was an oil-cloth covered counter behind a flap that opened up, racks for cups, deep trays for all the goods we would carry, cupboards for oddments, shelves for cakes. You washed up in a bucket at each stop.

The dry snow from our boots melted on the floor and trickled a little way, to freeze before it ran out on to the step. I slipped on that too on my next trip.

'Push the jugs in beside that bucket,' said Belinda. 'Three urns, aren't there? Can you see if the cup racks are full? Cups clean? Some cads *will* leave them dirty.'

There seemed to be enough cups for a regiment and Belinda said we only had to get the cakes and the cash and the dishcloths. So back we went into the hall, and Belinda bagged a couple of cake trays.

'Just fill these. Twenty dozen cakes to each urn,' she said. 'Buns, pastries, choc rolls, pies … Count them, will you, while I get the cash box.'

It took quite a time to count sixty dozen assorted cakes, to pick them out of the racks without leaving fingerprints on the tops, or getting jam on my hands, or crumbling the corners … I stood back at last and licked my thumb and watched the experts picking out half a dozen at a time and adding them up with a flick of the fingers.

Most of them were youngish, and nearly all were slim. Most of the uniforms were shabby; you can't serve hundreds of cups of tea without some spills; you can't continually climb in and out of a cramped driving-seat without creasing your skirt; you can't be out in all weathers, dodging from the wheel to the urns in a downpour without damping the smartness of the most expensive cap. But though there wasn't any glamour about these hard-worn uniforms, many of the faces were almost familiar; I felt that either I had seen them in the glossy pages of the *Tatler*, or else I soon would. Some, perhaps, had titles; all at any rate had homes and incomes; if they hadn't, they couldn't have afforded to come day after day – five days a week, some of them – to staff the tea-cars which had carried tea, cakes, chocolate, cigarettes and soap to balloons and gun-sites ever since the war began, and, in the blitz, had indomitably gone out to take food and hot drinks to the rescue parties and the firemen and homeless.

'It's always such a rush in the mornings,' said an earnest woman who seemed to be immobile and have the job of checking stores. 'This your first day? You'll soon get used to it. But you want to get *off*.'

'I'm waiting for my driver.'

'You'll love the work,' she said. 'I'm sure you will. All our workers do; they never miss a day if they can help it. Six hundred cups of tea, some of them serve; after all, I always say it's not so much the cup of tea that counts, but the smile with which it's given.'

She fixed me with a brilliant eye and I felt a little self-conscious, as if I ought to begin practising my smile at once.

Belinda came back with cash box and the dishcloths and whisked me out to the van. We made another couple of trips in and out with cakes and trays of cigarettes and soap and matches and shoe polish and writing paper, and I felt I was growing a new chilblain between each.

Every time we passed the earnest woman, she told us we ought to be gone long ago; perhaps she kept a log-book and wanted to show that all vans had left almost before the drivers had arrived, just as we liked to prove that no ambulance could take more than a minute to start on a call.

'We *are* off,' said Belinda at last. 'Not,' she added as she fastened the back doors with a bit of string because the catch was broken, 'that there's nearly as much hurry as she thinks. Voluntary women always *are* in a hurry, have you noticed?'

I said I had.

'It's the same thing with nurses; the real ones look slow and are quick ...'

'And the amateurs look quick and drop things ...'

'Like bad drivers – always starting off in a cloud of smoke ... Sorry, she does skid,' said Belinda as we slid away. 'The snow's funny; sometimes it's slush and some places it's ice.'

Not even the snow could make the East End look picturesque, or hide its scars; the whiteness only emphasised the thickness of the smoke, the ugliness of factory and gasometer, and stingy alley, the murk of railway arches, the crumbled devastation left by bombs. People looked pinched; you were sure they hadn't got enough clothes or enough food or enough warmth and you felt bad. By the kerb, horses steamed patiently, heads lowered, and we slithered on the tramlines behind more heavy horse-drawn trucks, the animals contending valiantly for every slippery step. Among the ruins, demolition men worked slowly, as if the cold made everything twice as heavy.

'Haven't been down this way for ages,' said Belinda. 'Just squint at the map, darling ... Not since the time they dive-bombed us. Of course it wasn't us really – but it felt exactly as if we were being personally chased ... I certainly stepped on the gas that time.'

'I think you turn left here,' I said, holding the sketch map upside down for luck.

'That's right,' Belinda agreed. 'By those gates ... I remember: I nearly lost all my cups there. It used to be a regular target, and headquarters said if the sirens went, I'd have to pack up and clear out on the first wail. All very well, saying that. But I'd a couple of hundred cups out and headquarters would have *slain* me if I'd come away without them. I'd have gone cuckoo, trying to get them back, anyway ... blokes who'd just paid a penny for their tea weren't going to pour the stuff away so I could pack up.'

'Did you stop for sirens at first?'

'You bet your sweet life we didn't. Some days, we wouldn't have sold a cup of tea if we'd paid any attention. Fourteen raids in a day ... that was before your time ...'

'I know … I missed the worst,' I said.

'Some places we went to, they had a spotter,' said Belinda. 'You carried on till he blew his whistle. Then you took cover – if there was any. Once the bomb came down just as he let the whistle go. But it missed. So he had a cup of tea on the house.'

She sighed. 'It's so *tame* now,' she said, turning down a side alley, bouncing a pavement and charging at an iron gate guarded by a sentry complete with fixed bayonet.

We were on the gun-site. It was an etching in black and white; the football ground sprouted guns and predictors; old cricket pavilions were brambled with barbed wire. We span a halt circle on ice. The wheels whirred, the engine boiled. Nissen huts disgorged hundreds of men; they plunged towards us, some wags hurling an odd snowball; then the van shuddered forward to the shock of twenty shoulders, and we rattled down a gritty path between latrines to a square where children's swings had once been slung.

There was a queue waiting for us; as we got the shutter up, mittened hands thrust tin pannikins, outsize mugs and metal soup bowls towards us. As I squeezed past Belinda to get at the urns, I saw at once why Mobile Canteen women are slim and middling tall; any one as long as Penny would have ricked her neck, and any one fatter than me would have stuck for the duration between the urns and the shelves.

I grabbed the pannikins; you only had to push them under the tap and turn it on, for the tea was sugared and milked. But you had to see that you turned the tap off in time, that you didn't twiddle it too far and jam it open. We sold tea not by the cup but by

You only had to put them under the tap …

the threepennorth or fourpennorth, pushing the steaming tins across the counter and hoping the last farthing's worth of tea wouldn't slop among the cakes. It often did; I hoped Belinda didn't see.

There was no time to talk, no time to watch, certainly: no time to smile, as you turned the tap on and off and mopped up the spills and reached for the mugs. But maybe the tea did quite well.

We hardly saw the red-brown faces, hazed by steam, as the queue shuffled past, and when the last man and the last bun had disappeared, Belinda slammed the shutter down, tucked away the cash box, helped me lift the urn to the floor and ran back to the driver's seat, flapping her arms like a demented duck. I got in beside her and sucked my cold fingers.

'We *could* go straight back,' said Belinda. 'It's late ...'

'Just as you say,' I said, blowing on my hands.

'It's pretty damn' cold, but I don't like to leave the balloon out. They do count on us.'

So we sidled out over the ice and down the back roads, the jugs awash and the tea cups rattling as we checked a broadside skid and set to partners with a lamp-post, bumped down a once muddy lane, under railway arches across a single track line, swaying on the edge of a frozen ditch as we skirted some forlorn allotments where the snow made a mockery of the little huts, the piles of bean sticks, the untidy potato clamps, the few poor sprouts rimed with sooty frost.

'Gee, sister, it sure is good to see you. Haven't set eyes. on a human for three days ...' That was the sergeant at the balloon site, a large and cheerful man in a leather jerkin.

'Kin you post a couple letters, baby?'

'Got any shaving soap?'

It wasn't just the tea that these men wanted, or even the oddments we sold them, but the company, the chance of a chat, the link-up with ordinary life that often seemed far away.

When we got back to headquarters, we hauled out the empty urns and dumped them on the pavement. We dried all the cups properly and stacked them away and swept up the crumbs and wiped up all the spills and went over the floor with a squeegee that smelt of sour milk. Then we took in the cash box and got a receipt for it and filled in some forms saying how many cakes we'd taken out and how many we'd brought back and then we wondered about lunch.

I said how about some cheap dive, and Belinda said she didn't feel like a cheap dive, and how about the Savoy? I said no because I only had half a crown and three half-pennies, but Belinda said it didn't matter, because her husband had just sent her a present and she certainly felt like the Savoy.

We got quite a kick out of taking our shabby uniforms into its grandeur, and feeling our hefty shoes, soaked with spilt tea, sink into its carpets, and relaxing on to its deeply cushioned chairs. We got rather more than a kick out of a cocktail and the sort of lunch, complete with hors d'oeuvres and chicken and sweets with synthetic cream, that the Savoy could still serve. But I don't suppose that lunch really tasted as good to us as the tea and buns we had doled out tasted to the men at the gun-site that morning.

After that, I often used to go out with Belinda on her rounds. Sometimes it was very cold and sometimes it was very wet and then Belinda would say what a couple of fools we were to go and get soaked and frozen taking tea to a lot of toughs who would be better without it. Sometimes, when the spring air was soft, we felt very limp and we couldn't get the smell of stale tea out of our nostrils. Sometimes we did balloon sites; there were a good many regular rounds, taking in all the isolated sites, and we tracked them down, in playing fields, in parks I'd never heard of, and in the old gardens of bombed houses.

Every balloon site seemed to have its own dog, which gave tongue when we appeared and strolled up to beg for biscuits as the men drifted towards us from the huts or the odd square of kitchen garden. Generally we had cups of tea too, leaning our elbows on the counter and talking about the best kinds of early peas and the news from the Balkans and worm powders for dogs and the prospects of leave.

Women porters.

Sometimes we went down to the docks or to goods yards, where we served tea to a gang of men and women porters; they came across in ones and twos, straightening their shoulders, mopping their faces, the men jerking on a coat, the girls tweaking out curls, slapping the dust off their trousers.

'Tea? You bet your life we could do with tea.'

'Tea and two pies twice, miss …'

'Can yer spare another pie fer my mate?'

The clamour of trucks shunting in and out, the clang of machinery being unloaded, the clatter of crates, the fizzing of a little steam crane, the thud of sacks on the stone platforms, the cheerful whistle of an engine pulling out, the put-put of a motor-driven trolley, all the brazen, healthy noises of the city's supply system, pulsing into action, they were curiously refreshing after the devilish uproar of raids by day and by night.

And as the year ripened, we went more and more often to the Cadets waiting to be posted for training with the RAF, housed now in mammoth blocks of flats, ground and first floor windows blocked against blast, wearing the derelict air of luxury property taken over by the government. In the wide roads behind, a crowd of men would be drilling; as we drove up, they dismissed and great waves of Air Force blue would surge down the street and engulf the van.

Always Belinda jumped out, beaming at them as though they were each her special boy friend.

'Who'll get the shutter up?'

A dozen willing hands lifted the flap and hooked it back.

'Strong men wanted for the urns …'

There was a rush for the job.

'Pass out the old bucket, sister, and we'll rinse the old cup as we go along.'

We filled the bucket with tepid water and put it in the gutter and the boys rinsed their own cups and I dried the rims before I filled them up again, while the queue clamoured cheerfully for more cake.

'Got any slab cake, girls?'

'Six buns and two pies and a brace of choc rolls …'

'Sorry. Can't be done,' said Belinda. 'Fourpence worth of cake and your tea, that's all we can allow.'

'Have a heart, sister, it's years since breakfast.'

'Two teas and three rolls and a bun – what's the damage?'

'Glory, what's sevenpence halfpenny from two bob?' asked Belinda. They did the sum in chorus for her.

The blur of eager faces passed and re-passed, such eager boys' faces, each with a look of Toddy, something about a bumpy forehead, something about the tilt of a nose, the set of a chin … blue eyes that twinkled like his, brown eyes that were warm and wide as his, smiles that teased as his did, voices that echoed his voice. Oh well, if you couldn't feed your own son, at least you could give someone else's a cup of tea. Maybe most of the older canteen women felt that way. And for the younger ones too, these strangers' faces mirrored a face they loved, and if they couldn't do anything for their own man, at least they could do some little thing for his friends.

Perhaps they would write home and say they were bored with slopping around and the food wasn't up to much, but there was a pretty decent canteen that buzzed up in the mornings. Perhaps somebody's mother would be glad to think there was a pretty decent canteen.

They were all passed fit for flying duties, all with the undimmed keenness of fledglings, all straining against the tedium of waiting and square-bashing.

'Say, I'm fed up, hanging about here ... you don't think this bloody war'll pack up before I'm posted, do you?'

Soon they would be gone ... soon they would get their wings ... soon they would be in action. It couldn't be soon enough for them.

Every time we went, there were new faces with the same smile, new voices echoing the same thoughts.

Always, as we drove back, Belinda would get out a cigarette and light up and smoke it very fast, and for quite a time she wouldn't talk at all.

X March, 1941

As the days lengthened, so the blitz receded, leaving us feeling like old elastic which has been strained so taut that it can't snap back to normal. At first it was a relief not to be so tired, not to be so anxious about the devastation that might come to some city every night, not to fret to be in action. But quite soon, much, much sooner than you would have thought possible, a night without a siren became a commonplace.

Penny and Belinda and I no longer looked at each other and smiled seraphically and sighed, 'another lovely night!' Belinda didn't stand by the window, listening to the distant rattle of the railway, and say, 'I'm so glad for the trains. I used to worry about them chugging away through the blitz.' Penny didn't say, 'Isn't it marvellous to think of all the people who can go to bed in peace? Isn't it grand to think that no one need be tired tomorrow?' And I didn't feel that queer, heart-warming thankfulness deep down inside me. We just went to bed and grumbled because the bathwater was cold. Only Barky, trotting between the East End and the West, didn't seem to notice the lull at all.

An odd, stifling cafard settled down on us. Nothing seemed worthwhile any more. Before, the very checking of one's ambulance, oil, water, tyre pressure, lights, the memorising of street names and hospital entrances, the cleaning of one's gas-mask, had seemed important because just possibly somebody's life might depend on how you did it. Now, nothing mattered. It was, quite suddenly, impossible to believe that we had ever been out, that the road had ever been pitted with craters, that the ruins round us had been made by bombs, that the clumsy ambulances had ever carried a casualty, that the blankets had ever come back filthy and bloodstained, that the First Aid bags had ever been opened by nervous fumbling fingers in the light of a hooded torch.

'What's the sense?' we said about everything.

'What's the use?'

'Who cares?'

We began to scamp cleaning the ambulances. What was the sense when we couldn't go out? We gave up practising First Aid. What was the point when we'd never need it? We grudged standing out on patrol in an east wind: we detested all the silly little details of forms and formalities. Maybe there would be a raspberry coming to us – who cared?

'I'm sure I should be ashamed of taking my pay and doing as little work as you,' said Mrs Boxer acidly when we'd lost three blankets and forgotten to check the gas suits.

'Charwomen's pay – we do the charring, don't we?'

'Well, you're only unskilled labour – what d'you expect?'

That's what we felt like, that's what we were – unskilled labour.

'I guess we're not as much use as lavatory attendants – and we don't get their tips either,' said Robin.

All the glory had gone from us – and we missed it. We talked rather often of the better jobs we could get, the really useful jobs with more work and more pay. On telephone duty, in the first hours of the cold mornings, we huddled in rugs, propping our eyelids open, cold with the chill of weariness, bored with the intolerable boredom which comes when one is compelled to follow the routine of danger in a time of utter inertia. And we, who had gladly forgotten our differences, merged our personal lives into the single purpose of saving others, shrank back into our own petty individualities, sparring, quarrelling, complaining.

On telephone duty in the small hours.

'I guess Greeny had no right to speak to me the way she did, just because I didn't go right out and help her clean.'

'Robin's impossible; she doesn't do a thing except drink coffee and play cards and leave her chores to me.'

'It's not fair, the way I'm always stuck on an hour's patrol – and then Mark never bothers to come and relieve me …' That was Bilson, going warily about her work, her chin cocked at a pugilistic angle, guarding her rights, she who, a few weeks ago, would have done anything for anyone without being asked.

'I hate the job, I hate the place, I hate everybody,' wailed Penny, who had simply loathed the days she wasn't working when the blitz was bad.

'My indigestion …'

'My headache …'

'My neuritis …'

'My cough …'

All the little ailments that had been forgotten, all the silly grudges that had been buried, all the small miseries of boy friends who didn't phone, of children who were tiresome, of cigarettes one couldn't buy, of letters and cables that didn't come, of shopping that was wearisome, all the big anxieties about our men, they blanketed our hopes, our longing to be useful, our affection for each other, our love for our country, till we paced up and down like moth-eaten animals in a zoo.

'Maybe it's the same for everybody,' said Robin with a saving spark of sense. 'I guess the rescue parties and the stretcher bearers and the wardens feel just as bad.'

'I wish to high heaven,' said Mark, 'that somebody would give us something to do.'

But nobody did. Instead they suddenly came and inspected us, discovered that we hadn't any shelter, clucked with concern, and built us one. We didn't take to it; they built it inside our common room, cutting off the floor space so the ping-pong was ruined and the women had nowhere to sit. It was a messy job; we had workmen and wet mortar and sore throats for weeks.

'Catch me going in there,' said Mark, sniffing the dank air, when it was finished.

'It's very good,' the ASO said. 'It's quite the proper thing for blast.'

We said nothing.

'Perhaps,' said the shift-leader, 'it's gas proof?'

We brightened. Perhaps it was.

But it wasn't.

'It'll do very well for the women to sleep in,' said the ASO. 'Or we could keep the rubbish there?'

We refused to be interested in shelters, or even in the possibility of gas. When a new course started, we listened apathetically to the lectures on arsine and mustard spray; we couldn't be bothered with the decontamination of vehicles and buildings, and were only faintly interested in the decontamination of ourselves.

Still, we cheered up a little when we were allowed to go in parties to inspect gas cleansing centres, because at least it meant being off the Station for a time, though we were repelled by the draughty, corrugated iron entrance, with its tray of bleach for the feet, the windy undressing room with its bins, and the cold passage leading to the showers, and the dressing-room where you would sit wrapped in a blanket till your Station Officer saw fit to send a rescue party with a suitcase of clothes.

'What's the big idea?' said Greeny, shivering. 'If we don't die of gas do we die of pneumonia?'

The Red Cross Commandant in charge said bracingly that she had been through the treatment in a bathing suit and a snowstorm and emerged none the worse.

'I'm sorriest for the undresser,' said Penny. 'Think of it, think of standing in that cold, peeling people's clothes off in a gas-mask ...'

'You sweat in gas clothing, even in a frost,' said Greeny.

'Well then,' said Penny, 'just imagine having to stand about with mustard fumes all round, wondering if your respirator leaked ...'

'Think of waiting all through the blitz to do gas and never having a chance to cope,' I said.

'Gee,' said Robin suddenly, 'say, how do I get here if I'm contaminated? Do I have to leave my car miles away and *walk*?'

We all looked at her. We didn't fancy walking, not in gas clothing and rubber boots.

'Let's find a place where they decontaminate Personnel and Vehicles,' said Penny. 'Come on, Gibsy, you've got the list of places … there's one quite near.'

'Bombed out,' said Robin.

'There's another … other side of the main road,' I said. 'Let's go.'

We went; it was an inconspicuous place in a yard near where the dust carts lived. We rang a bell and a plump attendant in ARP uniform let us in. He'd been in charge of it for two years, and he still kidded himself there might be a gas bomb any minute.

'Just the weather for gas,' he said cheerfully as he showed us round.

It was a grand place, not nearly as cold as the others; the showers were magnificent; the dressing-rooms spacious.

'This is much better,' said Penny approvingly, beaming on the attendant as if he were the favoured manager of the hotel she had selected. 'If there's gas I shall certainly come straight here.'

'That's right, miss. Pleased to see you, I'm sure. *We* don't mind, if you don't.'

'How d'you mean, *mind*?' said Penny anxiously.

'Men only, miss. But don't let a little thing like that put you off. You're not going to tell me you're *shy*.'

'Isn't that just like life?' said Penny when we got outside. 'Fancy having to choose between your skin and your modesty.'

'I guess I'm not modest,' Robin said.

Greeny and I weren't so sure; we went thoughtfully back to tea at the Station and read our text-books half the night, working out how long your gas suit would keep gas out.

As we came off the shift next morning, yawning with boredom, looking almost with loathing at the bus loads of office workers and factory workers, envying ATS and WAAF and WRNS because at least they had something to do, even if it was only cooking or clerking, almost envying the ladies in the Sherwood green of the WVS because at least they were busy with canteens or savings campaigns or old clothes and, anyway, they weren't compelled to do whatever they were doing, we saw a very frail, very elderly woman in a very good fur coat wheeling a pram.

It was an extraordinary shabby pram, and it had an old mirror in it, two kettles and a pair of boots.

'Perhaps she's moving house and can't get a van,' I said.

'Perhaps she's mad,' whispered Penny. But as we came abreast of her, she turned and peered earnestly at us and said:

'Have you got any old tins, old keys, old saucepans, kettles, bits and pieces?'

'Nothing that would be any good to you.'

'But I'm sure you have a great many things put away,' said the lady. 'Things you'll never use again. Have you ever thought seriously about *salvage*?'

Penny looked almost as embarrassed as if she'd been asked to think seriously about salvation.

'I never burn paper,' she said. 'All our scraps go to pigs … the borough's pigs … five hundred pigs …'

'But have you ever thought of the metals … the metal on old trinkets, and ornaments, the old keys … old trays?'

The Salvage shop.

Penny fidgeted; she was a human magpie; I knew quite well that she had a junk-room crammed with odds and ends. 'Oh dear,' she said. 'You make me feel quite uncomfortable.'

'Do you know,' said the lady, pausing to wag a finger at us, 'd'you know how many aeroplanes, tanks, rifles, bullets we could turn out if Everybody took salvage *seriously*?'

Penny sighed; you could see her conscience hurting her.

'If you've much,' said the salvage lady, firmly, 'of course we could bring a couple of prams round to collect. But we'd sooner you brought it to the shop – just round the corner, between the newspapers and the fried fish. We're open till four.'

'I might – one day,' said Penny.

'I can see I shall have to *remind* you …'

'We'll bring it round to-day,' said Penny, obviously feeling that she stood more chance of keeping back a little junk if the salvage lady weren't actually on the doorstep with a pram.

An hour later, I found an exhausted, exasperated Penny crouching on the floor of the junk-room, surrounded by little heaps, shifting things from one to the other. One, the smallest, was all the things she could definitely bear to part with; the middle one was all the things she couldn't decide about, and the biggest was all the things that on second and third thoughts she was sure would come in useful yet.

'Darling,' I said, whipping up a repulsive metal ink-stand that had been presented to someone by a corporation. 'You couldn't possibly want to keep that.'

'It has Associations,' Penny sighed. 'Everything has. You don't understand at all, Mildred.'

I packed Penny off to bed, and while she was asleep, I shook all the junk I dared into a dust sheet, wrapped up a parcel of old clothes that had shrunk out of all relation to Penny's figure, and staggered round to the shop.

There was a row of bins marked Bones, Clean Paper and Tins outside, and in its small window was a display of old-fashioned trinkets, beaded vanity bags, bits of embroidery and shabby samplers, selling for a few pence in aid of the Spitfire Fund. Inside, were two more elderly ladies, sorting junk beside a very smelly oil stove. Wafts of fried fish mingled with the smell of the stove, the aroma of mothballs, dirty clothes, musty paper and bones. One of the old ladies wore a WVS hat perched in a queenly way on her top-knot; the other wore an armlet round the sleeve of a shabby coat; they both wore several scarves and mittens.

'Dear me,' they said. 'What a big bundle. How very nice that is. And a new face too. We do like to teach people like yourself how very, very important salvage is.'

'I hope I've brought the right sort of things …'

'Quite splendid … keys … an aluminium saucepan, too. And this copper thing … if you've any corks and bottles, you might bring them another time.'

The shop door opened and a broad smiling face peered round it.

'I just popped in with ever such a lovely lot of bones. My doggie buried them in the garden and I dug 'em all up.'

The ladies beamed. 'People are really getting interested,' they said. 'It's such a pleasure when people are interested; of course we go round and call and have a chat … yes, the shop's open every day; several of us take it in turns, you know … well, it is a little chilly; but there, it's nice to be doing something useful, isn't it?'

It seemed to me a depressing little place, with its musty smell, all cluttered up with the discards of so many lives, all the kitchen things that had been gleefully bought, years back, when the owners first set up house, the odds and ends of finery, the trinkets which must once have been chosen with such care, wrapped in tissue paper and given as presents on birthdays and Christmas days. But the old ladies had more adventurous minds.

'So interesting, you know, to think that this old pan and that old kettle will really be useful again, turned into a little bit of armour-plating on a tank …'

I nodded and rolled up my dust sheet, and as they didn't really want the old clothes, I took them down to the Central Depot, which apparently did.

It was remarkable, I thought, how thoroughly the WVS understood the art of infiltration. They not only had a vast rabbit warren of a London headquarters. but they were in on the ground floor of every local activity. In almost every borough they were busy at the invitation of the town clerk, producing ARP wardens, organising canteens and welfare workers and clubs for refugees and Third Line Rest Centres and evacuation and camouflage netting depots and day nurseries for children, let alone salvage and saving drives and knitting groups and the housewives' service for being neighbourly in raids. And of course they ran endless committees.

It's always easy to make fun of committees, because of all one's aunts who sit on them and come back clucking that Mrs So-and-So is quite intolerable, the mothers-in-law who take the chair (though deaf and obstinate and immune from reason and argument). But you can't laugh at the work the committees do.

Committees.

I arrived by mistake, for instance, at one of the emergency homes for children, housed in a lovely Mayfair mansion, where under-fives from the East End are collected and sorted out before being evacuated, taken in and bathed and clothed and played with; a happy place, run by young, much-certificated nurses and older, motherly ones, where children screaming for their mothers one minute are bewitched by kindness and new toys the next.

And the Clothing Depot, when I finally located it, was pretty remarkable too. It operated in a building of imperial magnificence, where titles and ambassadors, celebrities of arts and letters and science, must have sipped champagne and applauded good music and discussed affairs of state in the dim alcoves. And now the parquet floors were callously scraped by heavy shoes and packing cases, as sensibly dressed WVS ladies, overalled and mittened, mostly hatted, because they belonged to a generation that likes to live – if not to sleep – in its hat, bustled about, packing and unpacking, counting and re-counting, losing and finding, and finally stacking clothes on the enormous shelves which reached to the painted ceilings. The elaborate chandeliers looked down on trestle tables piled high with men's vests and pants, women's knickers and blouses, children's suits and frocks, and the panelled walls, muffled by all these clothes, listened to the shrill voices of ladies counting and commenting.

'Five dozen men's vests … five dozen pants, large …'

'Twelve dozen shirts, flannel …'

'Now where did I put my specs?'

'Sixteen dozen shirts, cotton … oh dear me, who's taken my pencil …'

'Have you heard from your dear boys lately?'

'… my nephew in India …'

'Sixteen dozen …'

'My daughter in Malay …'

'Did I say sixteen dozen …'

'The climate … so trying for the poor men …'

'Yes, my dear, I said sixteen dozen quite distinctly …'

Rooms full of men's suits, of men's mackintoshes, of boys' shirts, of babies' woollies, or women's undies … new clothes and old clothes.

'Five hundred corsets, medium … five hundred corsets, large …'

Could there really be five hundred women large enough for those, I wondered, trailing through room after room with my bundle.

And in the great hall where the crates of clothing from America and Canada were unpacked, more women were waist-high in suits and dresses and children's outfits, all chosen with such care, packed with such skill, all to be counted and sorted into sizes and checked and entered in stock books before they were carried off to be piled away on shelves, in readiness for the next raid when they would be sent to replenish stock at the WVS depots where hundreds of people would be re-clothed in a few days.

It was a nightmare of packing and unpacking, a weird dream in which all the worst features of every removal, every family holiday, every exodus to school, were perpetuated on a mammoth scale.

'Such good work,' said the organiser, taking my bundle from me at last. 'We have such splendid helpers … they rarely miss a day. But of course we need more.' She looked thoughtfully at me. 'If people like you could give us a few hours …'

'I wouldn't be any use,' I bleated. 'I never could pack … never. My boy never got back to school with *all* his things.'

I ran very quickly away, assailed by the memory of Toddy's large trunk, as it had stood on the landing, with mounds of clothes beside it, as I counted laundry and desperately checked school lists, and sighed and said:

'Darling, I can't find your second footer shirt … I'll have to send it on,' and how Toddy had grinned with delight and said, 'You'll have matron after you, Muz.'

When I got back to Penny's house, she and Belinda were having sherry and there was another girl with them, a tall, slim creature with bright eyes and smooth black curls that touched her shoulders. Her lips were brilliant, and she looked as if she were perpetually surprised because she had pencilled her eyebrows in the wrong place. Her tin hat lay beside the waste-paper basket, and it had a W on it.

Her name was Elizabeth and they were talking about clothes too – new clothes – for she did fashion work when there was any to do. I didn't ever want to hear another word about clothes, but Penny and Belinda didn't feel that way. They hung on her words, watching her like greedy little puppies hoping for tit-bits.

Elizabeth said, 'Now if you want re-modelling, I can put you on to a woman who makes one's last year frock look a million dollars. What she's done to my old two-piece … it's a *miracle* …'

We clamoured for her name. But Elizabeth thought it would be best if we all came to dinner with her the next evening and saw it for ourselves. Only we must come early, because after supper she was on duty.

Her eyes sparked; her voice was pleased; clearly she didn't mind being on duty. Even if there was a lull, it wouldn't *last*, she said.

'Much trouble up your way?' Penny asked.

Elizabeth shook her head. A gas main had gone up that Sunday in December, and she'd been very cold indeed patrolling the road till the services came and roped it off and took charge of it.

'You people had all the trouble,' she pouted. 'In our sector nothing happened. Practically.'

She talked as though she'd been out hunting and had a poor run. She had that kind of courage; she'd like a good sporting country where the fences were stiff, and a horse that took a bit of riding. She took risks as a matter of course. You might crash out hunting, but you didn't let a little thing like that worry you. You might get hurt in a raid, but what did it matter anyway? You'd have your excitement first. She thought more of the thrill of hunting down incendiaries, spotting unexploded bombs, dodging HEs and scrambling in and out of other people's premises looking for damage than of the hurt that was done to people's lives. But then, she hadn't yet had to stand by, helpless, when people were dying, trapped in a cellar under her feet, or to watch stretcher parties carrying out casualties or see how people suffered as they lay in hospital, or how they mourned, yet stuck to their jobs.

We went to dinner at the boarding house where she stayed, tracking down the place through a wilderness of blacked-out streets. We were having soup at a round table with a wobbly leg, with Elizabeth and a couple of very young medical students, when the sirens suddenly went, and we all looked up at the sound. The boredom of weeks dropped from us: as our pulses jolted, we seemed to jump out of a cocoon of interia.

'I *said* the lull wouldn't last,' cried Elizabeth.

'They're passing over, just passing over,' said the older student, cocking an ear towards the window.

They were all wardens, and going on duty in the Post which was so conveniently situated in the basement of the boarding house.

'In fact,' said the younger student, 'we're on duty now – if anything happens. Which it won't.' He turned to his companion and began to talk picturesquely about the effect of blast on the human frame.

'The poor bloke's face was a sort of purple-black ...'

'The lung had collapsed completely?'

' ... haemoptysis, of course ...'

Penny, who never liked medical details, propped her chin on her hands so that her fingers covered her left ear, and talked indomitably to Elizabeth about clothes.

'Leg riddled with splinters, old boy,' said the youngest medical student. 'We operated right away ...'

'... you simply can't get a good crépe de chine,' said Penny firmly, kicking me under the table because horrors disagreed with her dinner.

'There's never anything doing in this sector,' said Elizabeth peevishly.

There was a clatter, as if the cook had suddenly gone mad and thrown every pan in the kitchen on to the floor and danced on the lot of them.

'*Incendiaries*?' cried Elizabeth as if she were giving a view hallo. 'Yes – incendiaries.'

She and the medical students got up so quickly that the floor quivered, the table tilted and the soup spilt over the cloth.

Penny and Belinda and I followed: Penny and Belinda really wanted to see the incendiaries, and I knew I ought to.

The youngest medical student was in charge and he had already popped into the street and back again.

'Dozen or so, up and down the road,' he said. 'I'll take the stirrup pump … Eliza, you can be number two … one of you women carry the bucket, will you? The rest of you, sandbags and what not. Look sharp.'

'You for the bucket,' said Penny. 'I don't like cold water splashing about.'

We were off; the medical student had one bucket and I hauled along two more while Elizabeth took the pump. As we went down the steps, the first spill of water splashed into my shoes.

The street looked like a firework display that had gone wrong, because the rockets had refused to leave the ground. They spluttered white against the shadows. We could see the others stalking them, one arm shielding their eyes, the other swinging the sandbag on to the flame. One by one the brilliant flares were quenched.

Our job was an incendiary that had lodged on someone's step and nestled against the door; the woodwork was blazing already. The medical student sprawled on the ground, with the nozzle of the pump in his hand; Elizabeth plunged the business end into the bucket and began to pump, her shoulders moving up and down, jerking at first, her breathing quick and excited, then settling down into a sharp, rhythmic swing. The spray drizzled on to the bomb, the jet squirted against the woodwork as the student swung it round; the spray drizzled, the jet squirted … the spray drizzled again …

'Water,' said Elizabeth.

I gave her the full pail. It was funny: at first that baby fire was intensely dramatic: you saw it as a living malevolence, a personal red devil: your mind shot back, and you saw thousands of other red devils, burning secretly in empty offices, in unwatched warehouses, hidden behind the parapets of roofs, till suddenly they joined hands behind a wall of flame, and the City burned, and on the fire towers, on the pumps, on toppling blackened walls, men had been killed. Your mind shot forward, and you saw what might happen if you couldn't cope, heard wood crackling under the flames, so that you knew it had got a hold on floor boards, that it was devouring curtains and furniture, that the little rivulet of flame had become a torrent, crackling and roaring as water crackles and roars over a cataract, till it poured out and the molten heat engulfed you.

But then, as the prosaic hiss and drip of water quenched it, it was no longer exciting, but just rather dull and rather cold, and the darkness closed in, split now and then by the flash of guns, whose sound was so familiar that you scarcely heard them.

Smoke made my eyes sting.

'Water,' said Elizabeth again.

I tipped my other bucket into hers; a lot of it splashed up over her trousers and mine. I ran back to the house for more water, hoping I'd know which was the right front door; but the landlady trotted out and pushed a couple of pails at me. I pounded back, spilling a pint at every step. When I got to the place the fire was out. Elizabeth was packing up the pump and the medical student had gone in to the empty house to look in the attics for more trouble. But there wasn't any.

We soused the woodwork and the dead bomb with the rest of the water and mopped ourselves. Then we went back.

Penny and Belinda, looking as pleased as terriers who have been ratting, and the other medical student were already eating mince and rice.

Elizabeth looked at her plate and made a face. 'I shall want a second helping,' she said.

XI March, 1941

It was Penny's idea that we ought to see something of the other services, if only to know what we were missing; Greeny had heard a rumour that we should all be conscripted into the Ambulance Service for the duration and Penny said we must have a look at the holes we might jump to – if we decided to jump while we could.

Semaphore girl.

She saw a photograph of a girl in the River Emergency Service, extremely attractive in a peaked cap, waving a semaphore flag, and she conveniently remembered that she had an old admirer who was something or other at the Port of London Authority. If Penny were set adrift in a desert, she'd have an old admirer in the next oasis who'd 'do anything in the world for me, my dear.'

And having contrived to get this old admirer to the point of asking both of us to spend a day seeing the River Emergency Service – the ambulance afloat, Penny then had a chill and I had to go by myself.

'I don't really mind,' Penny said. 'I never was awfully fond of yachting. And you'll be quite all right – he's a lamb – he'll do you proud.'

I don't quite know who Penny had said we were, or what we were supposed to represent, but certainly Penny's old admirer did us proud. As Penny's hand wasn't there to be held, he didn't come himself, but he provided a most imposing, gold-braided escort, with a broad grin and a twinkle.

'We've got the launch at the far pier,' said the Escort, looking me over with the twinkle. 'We weren't quite sure how decrepit you were, and there's a bit of a drop at this one.'

I said I was a lot too decrepit to jump from piers to launches as I no longer bounced when dropped and wondered how Penny would like hearing that she'd been dated as a back number.

We skirted the Tower of London and dodged down by Billingsgate and the Escort put out a protective arm to prevent me slipping on the greasy cobbles. The faint March smell of spring that had been tantalising everyone for days was suddenly quenched by the stink of fish; porters in their odd round hats, gleaming with fish scales, phlegmatically loaded up lorries, but the vim and vigour and bustle of the place had been damped down by the blitz and business wasn't what it was.

All around was a devastated area; it hadn't the pathos of a wrecked street of little houses; there were no strips of bedding, no household oddments, ground down into the rubble; it hadn't the dignity of the ruined churches, whose arches still sprang upwards, embracing the sky in their span. But it was grimly reminiscent of the Capitol at Rome; here a shattered pillar, there the inlaid flooring of some reception hall, the battered grille of a gate, the marble tablet to some commercial magnate, a glimpse of central heating furnaces, the arch of a wine cellar, half an imposing portico rearing up from a six-inch wall. The dust and the smell of ruin lay thick on everything and on everyone who walked there, and you felt you were looking at the shattered memento of an economic age that was already as dead as Rome.

'That bit went in December – that lot caught it very early on …' The Escort knew the blitz history of every missing landmark.

We twisted in and out between great drays loaded with rubble, lorry-borne cranes, gangs with pickaxes and shovels, to a little wooden pier. A launch, grey painted, flying the Port of London Authority's flag was made fast there, the deck just about level with the pier.

'Can you make it?' the Escort asked, swinging aboard, to hold out the protective hand.

I thought I might; even though the gap between launch and pier was not quite constant, I could heave a leg over the rail, clutch a kind shoulder and duck into the cabin.

'It's a very special launch,' the Escort said, and explained that it was manned twenty-four hours out of every twenty-four entirely by volunteers. Twenty-eight of them took it in turns to provide a crew of four for each shift. They were middle-aged men, with heavy responsibilities and important jobs, but they looked like schoolboys on holiday, and the one with the shiny oil-streaked face who popped out of the engine room, with a screwdriver in one hand and a bit of waste in the other, looked exactly like Toddy, bent on taking his electric train to pieces.

It was steamily warm in the cabin, and everything shone; there wasn't a finger-mark on the brass that all good sailors have such a passion for, and the copper lamps would have put the handiest housemaid to shame.

'S'matter of fact,' said one of the crew, polisher in hand, 'I'm rather a dab at brass. Only don't let my wife know.'

She looked so trim, so altogether domesticated, that little launch, built to carry parties on the Broads, that you could hardly imagine she'd ever dodged bombs, zigzagging up and down the flame-bordered river in the blitz.

'One thing we don't carry – and that's a stirrup pump,' grinned the Escort. 'You just kick incendiaries overboard.'

I said I wished he'd tell me about the River Emergency Service because I didn't know a thing about it.

'We've been going ever since Munich,' he said. 'So you can't accuse us of not looking ahead. We used to have fourteen ambulance vessels, but it's been cut down a lot. We run to six now – five up-Thames pleasure steamers, and one sea-going vessel – she used to do the Clacton-Margate trips. From the Nore up to Teddington, that's our beat.'

'D'you keep *on* going up and down it?'

'Lord, no. The ships are moored – each is attached to a definite wharf. They go out from there when necessary. Each has its own doctor, three nursing sisters, fully trained, they are, and nine auxiliaries – well – First Aid workers really. Six stretcher bearers and the crew, all men.'

'You're really a floating First Aid Post?'

'That's the idea. Only we take stretcher cases. Thing is that if we get a packet of trouble down river, we can ship our cases aboard, and bring them right up stream – up to Oxford, if it comes to that. And, if it does mean keeping them aboard several hours, that isn't going to hurt because we've got a doctor, and all the necessary appliances – nurses who can give 'em really skilled care. In fact, they'll do better than they would do if we pushed 'em off more quickly. Pretty snug, these boats – but wait till we go aboard, and you'll see for yourself.'

We chugged cheerfully downstream: you could see the great rents in the sky-line where HE or fire had wrecked a warehouse or laid waste a network of streets: and yet, between the skeletons of wharf and mill, some little waterside terrace of elderly, prim houses, some white and green striped pub leaning out over the river, stood there untouched, not a pane of glass missing, not a tile cracked, linking the rich past with the unpredictable future.

And always little grey tugs, drawing a float, chugged busily up and down.

'Minesweepers,' said the Escort, dryly.

We tied up alongside an old river steamer, whose name must have figured on many a bill advertising cheap day excursions, trips to Southend or to Henley. Every Bank Holiday, she must have steamed up and down, gay awnings out, flags fluttering, pianos, gramophones and accordions, banjos and ukeleles strumming the tune of the moment, the reflection of the bobbing lanterns staining the bright ripples, laughter and voices beating across from bank to bank, till the riverside residents snorted at the vulgar trippers. Now she was drab and grey, and on her side were the words: AMBULANCE SHIP.

The Escort was over the rail before we made fast; I made a jump for it and stubbed my toe and wondered what the really decrepit did, and we went down into the wide-windowed saloon.

Penny's old admirer must have pitched a pretty tall tale about

Penny, for the staff were all lined up, men stretcher bearers on one side, nursing auxiliaries and Sisters on the other, as if someone grand were coming to inspect. I was introduced; I heard nobody's name, I just gathered that the older ones with the white cords on their shoulders and an extra dose of gold on the cap were the Sisters, and the others rankers, all drawn from the Civil Nursing Reserve, trained either by the Red Cross or St John's, holding First Aid and Home Nursing certificates and with at least fifty hours' experience in hospital.

It was odd to be visiting a sister service, calling for a cup of tea and a chat and not coming to do a job of work. You don't see people in the same perspective: a hedge of conventions and good manners shuts you out, and you don't get to know them as you would if you'd even spent a few hours washing up together, let alone a night in the blitz.

The Sister-in-charge was being very polite and kind, and the Escort said she'd tell Mrs er … er … all about the job, and we looked at each other, and went and sat down on a pile of stretchers.

The big saloon looked like a miniature hospital ward; on either side were two tiers of stretchers, fitted out with blankets, pillows and hot water bottles. The cupboards which had once held crockery and stores were packed with medical supplies. By the door hung the gas clothing; in the little lockers under the ceiling, made to hold the trippers' parcels and bunches of flowers, were tin hats and gas masks. The galley, where teas and beers and ices and sandwiches and buns and chocolate and cigarettes had once been sold, where pretty barmaids had chaffered with the lads of the village, and snubbed the impudent and flattered the elderly, was set out as a surgery, treatment tables laid out, with trays of lotions and sterile drums of dressings, forceps in spirit, capped jugs of sterile water, and assorted splints, while Thomas's splints were slung from hooks.

'I suppose you could cope with almost any injury?'

Sister said they could; Sister said they'd seen some fairly grim sights in their time, for all things were quiet now.

'How d'you get them on board?' I asked, thinking I wouldn't like to heave stretcher cases over the rail.

'Through the windows – with proper tackle. Some wharves are fitted up with special davits for lifting and lowering. And of course we've got tackle for getting cases up from ships' holds. You never know when you'll have to bring a case up from some place where you can't take a stretcher. I suppose you know roughly what we do? We reckon to cope with casualties up and down the river, bombed ships, wrecked barges, trouble at wharves or piers. And of course we work in with the land ARP. We send parties to places that are cut off from the mainland by broken bridges or wreckage and so on. There's a doctor and three trained Sisters to each ship, and nine auxiliaries – they get the usual ARP pay, same as you people do. And a pretty good uniform. We need it; we stick pretty close to the job. Four days on and two off, you know.'

'Four days on end – on board?' I asked. 'On the boat all the time?'

But they weren't; they were on the job aboard the ship from nine-thirty to about six-thirty, and then they were on call in their billets. If the siren went, they probably manned the ship at once, but if the blitz kept them up all night, they were allowed to put in sleep by day. It was humane.

'What'd happen if we had a siren now?' I asked.

'There are nine of us on; one Sister and three auxiliaries would be on duty in the galley – that's to say, they've got to stand by the ship and deal with casualties here, working under the doctor. Every nurse knows exactly what she has to do: one may be on hot bottles or teas, for cases of shock, another on blankets, another helping Sister with the steriliser. The other Sister and three auxiliaries would be in the saloon; they'd be ready to make up a landing party with the stretcher bearers.'

'So you don't stay put till the casualties come to you? You go out and bring them in.'

'We certainly do. That's the best part of it.'

Somebody made a cup of tea; the stretcher bearers, the Escort and the doctor had gone off somewhere, and the atmosphere thawed. Soon, as we stirred and sipped, someone said had I been through the blitz? And then we began to talk, as old soldiers do.

'Oh, it's all right when there's plenty to do …' said a pretty child who looked as if she'd just left school.

'It's not so good just standing by all night, with the stuff dropping pretty thick, and never a call coming in. You feel so useless …' That was one of the older ones, sombre-eyed and low-voiced.

'It can't ever be much fun on the river,' I said. 'Bang on the target.'

'Heck – I'd sooner be on the river than in a dug-out … I reckon it'd take a direct hit to do any real damage.'

'Give me a job with the landing party, every time. You can *see* what's coming …' That was a cheerful, plump young woman who looked as if she'd played a lot of hockey.

'What's the matter with a spot of personal danger anyway?' said a tough little Scot. 'It gives a spice to life.'

'She ought to know; she's been bombed out of her billets twice,' put in Sister.

'Remember the first night of all?' said a dark-haired girl with a hint of Yorkshire in her voice. 'Remember how we stood on the top deck that afternoon, watching the dog-fights over Croydon way? Champion it was. And then, later, when we saw the smoke … we just thought that's another Jerry done for …'

'… never guessed then what we'd see when the call came through to go down river …'

'We thought we'd put in somewhere and land. But we couldn't land: had to keep mid-stream. Will you ever forget those fires?'

'The heat of it … all the fire floats out … the steam when the hoses were turned on … it was tremendous …'

'Remember the poor devils, scrambling about on the barges … they'd got trapped between the fires … only thing they could do was to make for the river …'

'We picked them up from the barges and the little boats – one was just about under water, it'd got so many people in it … Some of them had kids tucked under their arms … and most of them had cats or dogs … remember the old girl with the parrot …'

'Called Sister names no nice bird would know …'

'And then, when we'd put them ashore further up stream, and your people had taken over, we came back to our moorings and we just had to wait all the rest of the night, with nothing to do but watch.'

' … that time the bomb came slap through the wharf just beyond us …'

'… the night St Thomas' was hit …'

'Were you there when there was that trouble in Chelsea and we sent a landing party? … the doctor was wanted to give injections … pretty hopeless, most of the cases I saw.'

'That night when we were sent down river to pick up about a hundred minor casualties, and bring them back to our own pier; the authorities wanted them evacuated at once. This street was pretty well choked with ARP ambulances … they got there almost before we left. And then we hung about the river for hours and hours … and came back empty. Every single man and woman refused to come because it meant leaving their own district.'

'Quite maddening … but I don't blame them,' said Sister. 'If you can't be let stick with your own people when there's trouble, it's a poor show.'

'The worst job I ever had was when we went out to that tug with the tea barge,' said the dark girl. 'Remember that? The barge'd got a direct hit, and the tug was pretty well shattered. I'll never forget going over it with doctor – looking for the two men. Pitch dark, and your feet kept slithering in a filthy mess – all that tea blown over everything – inches of it …'

'We never found the men,' said Sister, slowly. 'Just a mess where their bunks had been …'

'I'd be terrified on the river in a blitz,' I said.

'I couldn't be doing with a job on land, cooped up like that,' said Sister.

'But when the blitz isn't bad – like now,' I said. 'When there are days and nights with no raids worth speaking of, how d'you feel then?'

'About as bad as you,' said Sister. 'Only I expect we're luckier. For one thing, we can do much more intensive First Aid training – we've got the staff, and we need to keep up a pretty high standard. There are plenty of jobs on board ...'

'Brass to clean?'

'Well – yes. Spit and polish never hurts. And then we all learn semaphore and morse.'

'You mean you really can read signals?'

'If we couldn't we'd be pretty useless once we got out of touch with the ship. You don't have telephones aboard boats.'

'But it's not real work – not the work you came for.'

'We get that too. There's always something happening. You never know when some of the firemen will hurt themselves ... there are accidents enough on the wharves and barges, and sometimes we go out to meet a ship that's come through the Channel ... been bombed or mined, maybe ... and got casualties on board. Then doctor takes a Sister and an auxiliary or two to lend a hand.'

Afterwards I said to the only Sister who was comfortingly grey-haired that they seemed awfully young, these girls who worked with her, on a job that was so often dramatic and so often dull.

Average age about eighteen to twenty-eight, she agreed.

'But you need to be fairly young and fit for this,' she said. 'It's an active job. When things are hot, you don't know what you'll have to get over or under, either on water or land. Our girls climb like cats. And when you have to go out to some ship with a casualty aboard, well you need to be pretty active to go up the side.'

Fairly young and fit.

'Er – you're pretty active, I gather?'

'Well,' she smiled. 'I spent a lot of time climbing out in Switzerland, every year before the war. That's why I can keep up with it.'

I nodded. No doubt if you've been up the face of Eiger or Jungfrau or the Dents du Midi, the steep side of a ship doesn't turn your head, and bombs are no worse than a blizzard at nightfall. You certainly had to be able to take a little excitement in the RES. We thought our job fairly arduous, our hours long. But I reckoned these girls had a tougher job than anything we'd had to tackle, and we could go home after a twenty-four hour bout of it, back to our own belongings and our comfortable beds (always supposing one's home was still where it always was). But these girls lived in billets. And billets are not like home.

Sister showed them to me; the staff lived in a block of LCC flats not far from the wharf; the men had one group of flats, the girls another. She did the communal housekeeping, and they'd made a dining-room, where they fed in relays because it wasn't big enough to hold more than six at a time, and quite cheerful common rooms. And the bedrooms were pleasant too; you thought how pretty they looked, each with different-patterned chintzes and ornaments and books about, and two beds, one in each corner. Then you looked at the beds: they were very fine camp beds.

'You have to be pretty tired to sleep well on a camp bed,' I said.

'We are pretty tired.'

Not every set of billets was as homelike as these; at another Station, all the women staff had taken over a ward in a hospital near the river. They'd divided it roughly into three, by hanging up curtains and pushing cupboards together, but there was a dormitory air, and though there were big arm-chairs pulled up beside old-fashioned fireplaces there was never any privacy, never the feeling of having a place of your own.

'But we don't mind,' they said. 'There's always the two days off to look forward to. That's a lot more than you'd get in the ATS.'

'I suppose it is. But do you stick close to billets all the time you're off?'

They didn't have to. They could get leave for a bit of shopping or to play games in a recreation hall, or to work on an allotment, and sometimes they went to dances given by the AFS.

'Great pals, the AFS boys,' said Sister. 'That's one thing in this job, you make friends, real friends, with all sorts of people you might never have met.'

At this station they all fed in an old-fashioned pub, in an upstairs room with stuffed trout and wedding groups round the walls; when the blitz was very bad, they sometimes waited for a call in the dug-out, designed by Christopher Wren as a wine cellar. Bombs had fallen only a few feet away, but the massive arches had scarcely trembled.

'Still,' said Sister, 'if there's trouble, I'd sooner be on the river.'

'There's something *about* the river …'

They all felt that way; the river *meant* something to them; it wasn't just a water highway; you couldn't imagine ever getting to feel the same way about the Edgware Road. The river had a life of its own, a way of its own; the air above it tasted different; the wind that blew up it, with ice on its breath, felt more alive.

'Looks lovely now,' said Sister, as she took me back from the billets down the gang plank, sniffing the spring wind that fluttered the flag.

'It does. I should think you never get tired of the river; it always looks good.'

'After a bad night,' she said, turning thoughtfully to me, 'it looks like black treacle. Sometimes it doesn't do to look down into it. Then you think perhaps you'd sooner work on land, where casualties don't get drowned as well as bombed.'

'But you don't go,' I said.

'No, you don't go,' she agreed.

When I got home, Penny wanted to know if the RES would do for us. 'Because I'm getting sick of sitting about in that stuffy garage,' she said. 'I'm needing a change – it's the spring.'

'You any good on ladders?' I said.

Penny didn't think so.

'Or the long jump?'

Penny didn't think so either. 'Well, it seems to me,' I said, 'that you've got to be a pretty classy athlete for that service. You're always leaping on and off piers or barges, or going up rope ladders or what-not. Let alone being able to swim, in case people fall in.'

'Oh, dear,' said Penny. 'If I were ten years younger ...'

XII March, 1941

That spring, while things were quiet, Mark said she couldn't think how we could all be content to sit on our behinds doing nothing for forty-eight hours a week and spend all the others getting over the strain.

'People who think they are great little heroes just because they've been in the blitz,' she said, 'and want to slack for the rest of their lives – it makes me sick.'

'Who slacks?' said Towser sharply. 'I do a part-time job, typing for my old boss. Think I can live on the pay, and keep my kid sister?'

'Speak for yourself, Mark,' said Johnny. 'I drive a van three days a week. Good fun, and better pay than I make here.'

'I've got a family to look after,' said Robin. 'I guess it takes me all my time, queueing up to feed two great men.'

'I've got my garden,' said Bilson. 'If you call digging up a lawn doing nothing, come and try it.'

'I don't see why Gibsy doesn't do something extra,' said Penny suddenly. 'Mildred, I think you ought to. You haven't got any housekeeping.'

I opened my mouth to say I couldn't possibly. But I didn't like to; I remembered the book girl whose Red Cross Libraries were always short of good workers, and Mrs Dove who said her Canteen Ladies were giving in to flu in a way they didn't ought to, and Belinda whose Mobile Canteens could always use a good driver, and Barky who'd said only the other day that if people realised conditions in the East End the work wouldn't be half-paralysed for lack of helpers.

'You'd better get Mrs Dove to take you in hand at her canteen, Gibsy,' said Mark. 'Penny'll get a kick out of arranging that anyhow.'

'B-but I d-d-do an awful lot of washing up here,' I complained.

'I can see you're going to need keeping up to this,' said Penny. 'Never mind; I'll do it.'

Mrs Dove, consulted by Penny without my knowledge, looked me over in the kitchen that night.

'I don't rightly know if you'd be any use, Mrs Gibson,' she said. 'You've not had much experience, have you?'

'Well, I've run a house for donkey's years.'

'Beside, we've trained her very well at the Station,' said Penny. 'She serves suppers hot now.'

'Yes, but is she a *breaker*?' said Mrs Dove.

'Well, she is rather,' said Penny. 'Aren't you, Gibsy? But she always remembers to keep the bits, so that's okay by the LCC.'

'T'wouldn't do for us,' said Mrs Dove. 'We aren't government-run, Mrs Pennant. But I'll speak for you, Mrs Gibson,' she added kindly. 'Yes, I'll certainly speak for you tomorrow.'

Mrs Dove's canteen lived in two large houses in a terrace that had once been fashionable before it degenerated into the haunt of select private hotels, of the kind frequented by elderly uncles and aunts up for Christmas shopping.

In fact, I could remember going there to dinner with an uncle and aunt myself, soon after the last war. Now there was a large placard over the door saying BRITISH RESTAURANT, and outside the porch was a blackboard with the day's menu chalked up on it. Soup 2d. Mince and 2 veg 7d. Steamed pudding and jam sauce 2d. Tea 1d. Coffee 2d.

I went in, very timid, cursing Penny's talent for finding people jobs. And there was Mrs Dove, in a green overall with red lettering on it, standing by the line of stoves, with her arms crossed over her chest, sure sign, as Penny always said, that she herself was not going to be crossed at any price. Two youngish women in white coats and tall white chefs' hats were listening meekly to Mrs Dove's opinion of the mince.

'Mrs Dove supervises the cooking,' whispered a lean, dark-haired woman whose name I didn't catch, rolling up her sleeves. 'We're all a little in awe of Mrs Dove – but she's a magnificent cook – does all the catering too. I think perhaps you and I had better go away rather quickly and start on the potatoes if you don't mind. She doesn't like to see people hanging about.'

So we started in on the potatoes; they were heaped in enormous bowls on a long trestle table.

'The peeling machine's out of action – it usually is. You'd better find a knife.'

It took me some time to find a knife because whenever I picked one up and took it over to the table and put it down for a second while I reached for a potato or rolled up my sleeves, someone else with a knife problem annexed it. By the time I had grabbed a very blunt thing with a broken handle, about a dozen women of all shapes, sizes and ages were busy on the potatoes. Some were young and pretty, some were middle-aged and plain, some were almost old, with grey hair and pince-nez; some wore rubber gloves to protect their hands; some brought their own safety potato peelers; some wore brief flowered overalls, some wore long green ones that trailed to their ankles. But with the exception of Mrs Dove and a bustling young woman in horn rims who called everybody 'dear', they were mostly the sort of women who did not usually peel potatoes. Most of them, at any rate, were older and frailer than many women I knew who had fled from London to the country because their nerves would not stand the noise and they were really too delicate to be any use. Some of them would normally have spent their days in social flutters and gone home to butlers and ladies' maids, cooks and kitchen maids. It was hard to imagine any of them even existing without two in the kitchen. But they all peeled potatoes as if the war effort depended on it, and they certainly turned out four to my one.

If you've only cooked a family dinner, you just cannot visualise potato-peeling by the hundredweight. As soon as we'd finished one great bowl another two appeared on the table.

There were a lot of questions I wanted to ask, but it was almost impossible to talk, unless you muttered with your eyes on the job, or were such an expert that you didn't need to look at what you were doing. Even among the experts there wasn't much chat.

'Now, now, Mrs Gibson,' boomed Mrs Dove, over my shoulder. 'Can't you be a little quicker? We got to look sharp *here*, you know.'

I cut my hand being a little quicker and the next few potatoes were definitely pink.

'I don't think much of the new char,' said someone on my left. I blushed, but she didn't mean me, she meant one of the two women who were paid to do the worst washing up and the scrubbing of floors. They and the two cooks were the only paid staff in the place.

'... such smears she leaves on the plates ... and she never washed under the dresser. You'd think she could do better than that.'

'Oh well,' said my companion, 'she's *paid* to do it, poor thing. We do it because we want to, so of course we do it well.'

'When you come to think of it,' I said, battling with an obstinate potato that floundered out of my hands, 'I don't know how we'd get along in this war without the Voluntary Worker. And the poor wretch used to be a joke.'

'Gracious,' said Mrs Dove, looming up again. 'All thumbs to-day, Mrs G.'

I tied my spare handkerchief round my second cut and wondered if I'd have any thumbs left by closing time.

'Eleven-thirty – we'll have to lay tables,' said someone.

'However will the potatoes get cooked in time?' I asked.

'They're for tomorrow.'

The mince was simmering in enormous pans, and Mrs Dove was pacing up and down before the stoves, inspecting sauces, peering into giant steamers, opening and shutting ovens. The room reminded me a little of the Giant's Kitchen scenes from Jack and the Beanstalk. Huge thermos urns presented by the American Red Cross were waiting for tea and coffee and soup. It took two people to lift them. A man came in with six sacks of vegetables from Covent Garden and dumped them in a corner.

'Cabbages, I expect – for us to shred this afternoon.'

'Do we work this afternoon *too*?' I asked.

'Well, we only really *work* between twelve and two when we're serving,' said my little friend.

I wondered what on earth we'd been doing all the morning,

and if at first everyone's back had ached as much, their fingers gone numb, their legs felt as weary as mine. If so, they were certainly plucky, especially the older ones, to come again and again and again.

Mrs Dove and her assistant were whispering together.

'Don't put her on the washing-up, dear,' said Mrs Dove. 'At least, not on the glasses. They tell me she's a breaker.'

'She'd better serve.'

They beckoned to me: I was to serve soups in the second dining-room and I could stop potato peeling and go and help get ready. Mrs Hicks would show me.

People were drifting away from the potato table to their appointed tasks. A nice smiling woman in a big grey coat and a knitted hood went out to the cold cash-desk in the porch where customers bought the differently coloured tickets that entitled them to each course.

'I always do it,' she said. 'You see, I don't mind arithmetic, and besides I've a pair of my hubby's old flying boots I can wear.'

'Pink for soup to-day, Margaret, yellow for meat, blue for pudding ...'

Another grey-haired body toddled over to a side table and got herself a small tin bath of warm water.

'You serving?' she said to me. 'Tch, tch!' she shook her head. 'Ah, I never do that. As long as I can work in a corner by myself, I get through a lot. But people fuss me.' So she specialised in washing up the cutlery as a couple of youngsters collected it and brought it out.

Somebody else did the glasses, somebody else gave the paid chars a hand in the scullery, for if there was a big rush, plates had to be washed up as we went along. There were two big deep sinks in the scullery, and the taps and hose-pipe attachments for filling the urns.

Each of the two dining-rooms had its own servers, two people on soup and meat and veg, one on sweets and one on tea or coffee, and someone to collect the used crockery from the table by the door where the customers parked it.

Mrs Dove was handing out glass cloths, one for each server for wiping rims and holding hot plates, and one for each dish so that it could be kept covered from the air.

Mrs Hicks, large and amiable, dark hair just showing silver here and there, was lighting the hot plate. It was an enormous thing, with cupboards for plates. She stooped with a grunt to reach the burners.

'Stooping's good for my waist,' she said. 'But my knees creak a bit, getting up. Probably good for them, too. Just bring in about a hundred plates, would you?'

I never knew before what awkward things plates could be.

'Tut, tut,' said Mrs Dove, as I wobbled out with a pile, wedging my chin on the top one.

The dining-rooms were quite gay; the old hotel paper of trellises and roses matched the check tablecloths and there were flowers on the tables, blue bowls of daffodil bulbs and

I never knew before what awkward things plates could be.

one of scyllas. There were boxes on the window sills marked 'Donations for Flowers'. They rattled cheerfully when I picked them up.

We trotted in and out, bringing up plates and fetching enamel dishes of mince, of potatoes, of greens.

'Twenty portions to each dish,' said Mrs Hicks. 'When there's a moment's peace you have to count the tickets – just get a pudding basin for people to pop them in, will you – we must be sure we're not being too generous.'

Mrs Dove called to me to fetch my giant thermos of soup, and as I staggered out with it the first customer came in. We were open.

For the next twenty minutes I could hardly look at the customers' faces, I was so anxious to see if they had a pink ticket among the fistful of yellow and blue ones. If they had, they wanted soup, and I'd open up the thermos and plunge in the ladle and fill up the plate. At first I always knocked the lid on to the floor and filled the ladle too full and the soup slopped over and then I'd find myself standing in a greasy puddle with a queue forming behind me. But after about fifty soups I began to get the technique taped.

When it wasn't soup it was vegetables, a big enamel spoonful of potato and another of greens, plopped at exactly the right moment into a plateful of mince. If you missed the moment, you had a spill. After a bit the hot plate began to smell a little of fried potato and Mrs Hicks passed me over a dishcloth.

'You don't need to be in *quite* such a hurry,' she said.

She didn't seem to be in a hurry at all; apparently she could not only see her customers but smile at them and talk to them as well.

'No soup for you, sir?' she said to a shabby bowler-hatted clerk. 'But it's very good. Just the thing to keep out an east wind.'

'... very little potato for you, madam? *You* don't need to bant with your figure ... And how are you keeping, madam? We haven't seen you for quite a while ...'

'I bin away fer a bit of a 'oliday,' said the stout, rather bronchial woman in a purple hat and a fur tippet. 'After the last blitz, see? 'Ad me kitchen roof blown off in that one ... not a dish nor a plate nor a cup left, I 'adn't. So I bin down to me sister in the country fer a bit of a rest. Come back yesterday ... put a roof on me kitchen, they 'ave, but the gas 'asn't come on yet.'

'When we first opened,' said Mrs Hicks when madam had collected her mince and two veg, 'a lot of streets round about had no gas. We served four hundred lunches every day for a fortnight ... felt we were being really useful then ... of course, now, we don't get quite so many. It's not really the same in a lull ... And what can we do for you, sir?'

Porters from the goods yard, rescue men, stretcher bearers, little clerks from offices nearby, lorry drivers, mechanics, typists shivering in their smart thin coats, shabbier women from the poor streets by the railway, old ladies who couldn't cook frugal meals any longer on their gas rings in their one-room homes, mothers with squalling children, she had a smile and a word for each of them, and they were all Sir and Madam to her.

At the far end there were two long tables marked "Reserved for Children"; presently a tail of small boys and girls came in, a twelve-year-old in long patched pants in charge of two spindly-legged little creatures, patiently choosing the lunch for them, shepherding them to the table, mashing the food down with a fork, scolding them when they spilt.

'Kids from the school round the corner – the mothers are on munitions – they eat as much as two grown-ups, but we charge them half-price. Ought to be in the country – but they won't go.'

Their high squeaky voices shrilled.

'I got a footer game 'safternoon. Match. I'm goal.'

'Goo – that's nothing. I was centre-forward las' week.'

'Get us another go of puddin' ... I bin twice already.'

By one o'clock, we had served sixty lunches and I had made two trips to the kitchen for fresh supplies. By half-past, I could lean back occasionally and let the service table behind me take a little of my weight.

Then a scrubby, middle-aged man, looking grey and cold, came up with a bunch of pink and yellow and blue tickets which he tossed into the pudding basin.

'Got somethin' good, miss?' he said. 'I risked a bob on this meal.'

'Smells awright, don't it?' he said, as I plunged my ladle deep into the thermos and filled his plate till it ran over. Mrs Hicks absently gave him two spoonfuls of mince.

He'd finished it in no time, fork clattering greedily against the plate, and we saw him go up to the other table for his pudding. He took longer over that, leaning back between mouthfuls, chewing slowly and thoughtfully as if he could spare time to taste the food.

When he'd had his tea he came over to us again.

'I'm obliged to you, miss,' he said hoarsely. 'When I come in yere, see, I felt downright queer. Fact is, I only come out of orspital yesterday. Bin in ever since that last day raid. Lorry driver I am. Ole lorry, she's done for. Not me, though. 'Itch 'iking back 'ome, I am, to-day. London man, but me 'ome's in Cardiff, see?'

'Good luck to you, sir,' said Mrs Hicks.

'I'd jest like to say thank you,' he said, turning away. 'A meal like that, well, it puts 'eart into a man.'

He was gone; the dining-room was empty now. We had stacked up the used dishes and counted the tickets …

'We're just over the hundred,' said Mrs Hicks. 'Not really a *busy* day.'

But suddenly all that cooking and potato peeling and washing up and sweating and aching was full of meaning: I didn't wonder any more why all these women bothered to come, steadily, two, three or four days a week, spoiling their hands and wearing out their feet and their shoes, fretting if they ever missed a day. They weren't just serving meals to fill bellies: they were serving meals that put heart into a man.

'Just take the empties through, will you?' said Mrs Hicks, 'and when you come back we'll clean up.'

It was quite an extensive clean up, too; first of all we wiped the fried potato and cabbage off the hot plate and then we greased it with vaseline. Then we swept up every crumb from the floor in our corner and mopped up every soupy puddle. Then we got soap and water and scrubbed the service tables. Then we got brooms and brushes and dustpans, shook the tablecloths out and folded them, and swept the entire floor.

By that time it was two-fifteen.

In the kitchen, Mrs Dove was standing by the one remaining dish of mince, ladle in hand. We formed into line with our plates and forks, got our portion and sidled away, eating as we went. Some people perched on tables, others flopped on to the sacks of cabbages, others pulled chairs up to the dining-room fire and toasted their cold and weary feet.

Two of the younger ones whispered in a corner; one of them massaged her hands with cream; she was going to a party – if the night was quiet – she had a friend home on leave. She would go home and get supper for her parents first.

'It'll feel funny to be in evening dress,' she said. 'Almost improper.'

They whispered again, giggling, and she blushed.

The older ones were quiet, slumping into themselves as they relaxed. One of them pulled out a bottle of pills and shook two into the palm of her hand.

'Have you tried Herbal Tea?' said another. 'I haven't had any rheumatism really since I took it.'

' … No, I haven't heard from my boy just lately … the mails from the Near East … they're very slow … Still, we mustn't complain.'

' … I like to keep busy … you don't notice how long there is between letters quite so much when you're busy …'

' … we ought to get on …'

After lunch, some of us helped the paid chars to clear up and stacked the clean crockery in the cupboards; others cleaned up round the stoves. And those who had been issued with dishcloths personally washed them through and hung them up to dry.

I caught sight of my dark-haired friend, standing over a sink, straightening her back for a moment. She tipped back her head and looked out at the sky, blue with puff-ball clouds, as though she hated it. A sky like that didn't mean the promise of spring – it meant good flying weather – and she had a son in the Air Force.

'Now for the cabbage, ladies,' said Mrs Dove. And we scrummed round for old knives again, and cabbages were tossed up on to the long table for us to shred.

Doing cabbages for two or three is not at all the same thing as doing them for hundreds. Your hands got very cold as you handled the greens, and your fingers grew corns.

She looked at the sky as if she hated it.

'You mustn't be so wasteful, Mrs Gibson; just cut out the stalk and the tougher fibres and shred the rest.'

A snail slimed over my hand.

Mrs Dove came round with a bowl and swept the shredded cabbage into it as we sliced.

I was too tired to listen to the conversation round me; all that mattered was keeping pace with the infernal bowl as it journeyed up the table, collecting shredded cabbage.

It was nearly four o'clock before we finished.

'I expect you're tired,' said my little dark-haired friend kindly.

'I am – a bit.'

'Ah – you'll get over that.'

'It's hard on the feet – but you get used to it,' said the elderly one who did the glasses.

'It's ruination to the hands … but still …' said the pretty young one.

'… my back used to ache … well, it still does, sometimes …'

'… my ankles used to swell …'

'You'll get used to it …'

'*And* it's well worth it.'

'Going home, Mrs Gibson?' said Mrs Dove. 'You've not done so badly.'

Back home, I lay flat on the floor, with my head on the hearth-rug and my feet on the sofa, waiting till they came back to their normal size so I could take off my shoes. Mrs Dove came in, aproned and calm – she overlooked my attitude and said:

'Would you fancy a little bit of plaice for your supper, madam?'

XIII April, 1941

We stood in the yard one morning, Penny and Mark and Robin and I, watching a huge grey AFS vehicle being fed with petrol from our pumps. It was Mark who strolled over and spoke to the girl sitting next to the driver.

'Come and look,' called Mark. 'We may. You've never seen anything like it – it's a proper kitchen.'

It was; there was a real coal range across one end, there was a big sink, with plenty of hot water, for they hauled hundreds of gallons in large tanks; there was a cupboard full of stores and rows and rows of pots and pans.

'Why, you could cook for a family,' Penny said.

'We cook for several hundred often enough,' said the girl. 'We get sent places where our people haven't proper canteens, or perhaps their cooking arrangements have been upset by a raid. And we just get down to it and feed them.'

She liked cooking, she said; and it was fun learning to cater for big numbers; but most of all she wanted to learn to drive canteens and kitchens; that way you went places and saw people and if the work was hard, it had the tang of adventure.

'Seriously,' said Penny, as the mobile kitchen drove sedately away, 'I think we ought to consider the AFS in case we want to change.'

Mark and Robin looked scandalised. Changing from one Civil Defence job to another was quite unheard of.

Mark said, 'I bet they don't really do any more than we do. It's just the lucky ones who pick on a job like mobile kitchens, and anyhow you can't boil a potato, let alone peel one.'

'We don't really know what they do,' insisted Penny. 'Now do we? We just think we ought to have their overcoats.'

'Who wants to know what they do?' Mark said.

'They may work a lot harder and do far more exciting things,' said Penny restlessly.

'Who wants to work a lot harder?' asked the shift-leader.

A round, amiable girl in AFS uniform.

'Because if it's you, Penny, you can go clean an unmanned ambulance.'

'I want a job where I feel I'm *doing* something,' said Penny recklessly. 'I don't care what I join – I shall volunteer for something tomorrow.'

'You're safe enough,' said Robin, sourly. 'They won't look at you.'

Of course Penny insisted that I was in this too. It was the easiest thing in the world; we would simply change into mufti and go and volunteer at the nearest Fire Station.

Penny looked very dazzling in mufti, in her green Schiaparelli hat with two silly little feathers in it, and she pounced on a round, amiable girl in AFS uniform who was standing by the Fire Station.

'I want to volunteer at once,' Penny said.

'I – I'll have to go and *ask*,' said the girl.

'This minute?' said Penny.

The girl backed towards the side entrance and we followed her. I could see Penny pining to go in and pat the fire engines and talk to the man on patrol; she didn't like being taken in by a back door and made to wait at the foot of an uncarpeted flight of stairs.

'She might have taken us up and introduced us, I do think,' said Penny.

'She's probably telling her officer that there are a couple of lunatics downstairs, and they'll put the hoses on us if we're tiresome.'

But another AFS girl beckoned us up the stairs and into an office where one young woman was sitting by the fire knitting while another was typing strenuously; she was extremely pretty and you couldn't help wondering if she'd been picked for the job because the uniform suited her so well. She said it was very good of us to come along, but – she didn't seem to take us very seriously. That was probably the fault of Penny's hat; you couldn't blame any one for thinking that she'd never done a stroke of work and would faint if she tried.

'What I want to know,' said Penny, who was quite clear in her mind that she was doing the country a service by volunteering. 'Is this: is it really useful work? Something where one's abilities would be used – not just sitting about knitting,' She glared at the girl by the fire.

'We always have *plenty* of work,' said the girl briskly. She looked reproachfully at Penny and then at the wire basket stacked with papers by her typewriter.

'Oh – office work,' Penny said ... 'I – er – I'

'We're not much good at office work,' I said.

'You aren't *cooks* are you by any chance?' said the girl with a gleam of interest.

We repudiated cooking.

'Well, I'm afraid I can't help you very much till you've been to the Labour Exchange. You should really have gone there first. You can't volunteer *seriously* without an ED 60, you know.'

'Oh dear,' said Penny. We looked at each other and got up to go.

At the door Penny turned to murmur, 'Er – an ED 60, you said?'

'ED 60,' said the girl cheerfully. 'A form, you know. And it must be filled in and signed before we can consider you.'

'Let's give it up,' I said. 'You know quite well that you aren't a cook or a shorthand typist, and I don't believe you'd be any use as a telephonist.'

'I'm superb as a telephonist,' Penny said. 'You know how good I am at saying I'm out when I'm in. Let's take a taxi.'

'Where to?'

'To the Labour Exchange,' said Penny firmly.

The Labour Exchange was in an ex-church hall; there were a great many notices in the porch and rather a queue. We stood in it for quite a long time, till at last a one-armed commissionaire came up and tapped Penny on the shoulder.

'Registering with the twenty-ones, are you?' he asked. 'Been twenty-one quite a time, meaning no offence.'

'We don't want to register,' I said. 'We want to get something called ED 60.'

'Upstairs,' he jerked his thumb over his shoulder. 'Keep yer pecker up – there ain't no age limit for munitions.'

Upstairs was bleak, filled with long ink-stained tables and clerks with colds in the head. We sat down beside one with a hacking cough and Penny said brightly, 'We're thinking of joining the AFS and we want you to give us ED 60.'

The girl blew her nose and wiped her eyes and whispered to another girl, who whispered to another, who finally produced a folder. It seemed to have a photograph of someone in AFS uniform by the side of typed particulars.

Our girl read bits of it aloud, very quickly … 'Auxiliary Fire Service … vacancies for women … telephonists, clerks, cooks … age limit fifty … unless you're cooks.'

'I am not fifty and I am not a cook,' said Penny. 'I want to be a driver.'

'You ought to join the Ambulance Service if you're drivers.'

'I said a *driver* – not a charwoman,' said Penny. 'I want to drive a fire engine or a tender or something.'

'It doesn't say anything about that here,' said the girl. 'Clerks, telephonists or cooks … but anyway you would require an ED 60.'

'I know that,' Penny said. 'Can't you hand it over?'

'I'll have to take all particulars,' said the girl.

'What? Age, nationality, mother's birthplace and grandfather's religion?' said Penny.

'And if you're in employment …'

'What if I am? I can give my notice, I should hope?'

'We might not release you to join the AFS,' said the girl primly. 'It depends on your employment …'

Penny leaned across the counter, out of temper and out of

breath. 'What's the penalty for wilfully giving false information on an ED 60?' she asked.

'Are these ladies giving you any terrouble?' said an acid voice, and a majestic figure in black with fountain pens clipped all over it, loomed across the room.

'Ay'm sure mey gels are only too glad to help you,' she said, standing over Penny, 'but mey gels are not here to answer frivolous inquiries ...'

'Is this all the encouragement I get when I want to volunteer?' demanded Penny, uncoiling to her full height.

'Are these ladies giving you any terrouble?'

'We can't help you to volunteer if you withhold information,' said the black majesty. 'Are you mobile or immobile?'

'Oh, immobile,' said Penny quickly. 'Very. I have a lot of trouble with my feet.'

After that no one would take us seriously; I slunk out behind Penny, whose Schiaparelli hat was still cocked at a defiant angle and stood Penny a film to take her mind off the AFS.

But there is no heading Penny off while there is something she really wants to do; when she got home she remembered that she had an old admirer who had a sister who was in the AFS. But really High Up in it; Penny wouldn't wonder if she weren't practically head of all the firewomen in England.

At any rate, the old admirer's sister arranged an appointment for us with an officer at Lambeth without mentioning ED 60; and this time we set off in sober tweeds: Penny's Schiaparelli hat had done enough mischief.

We viewed the headquarters of the Fire Service with approval; it was both austere and imposing. Penny nodded sagely; you could see she thought that work in a building like that would feel twice as useful as the same work in a back alley office.

We gave our names to the porter in the spacious hall and expected to be shot up in a lift to an ultra-modern office which would make a suitable setting for a superwoman in the AFS.

But we were asked to go through the yard to the block of flats behind. In the yard, we loitered, for every size and shape of fire appliance seemed to be coming in and out of it, and two or three girls swirled up in staff cars and parked them with one swoop in a rank at the back. Squads of men were pelting about with pumps and pipes and ladders, and more were scaling the high practice tower. In fact, a couple were just getting ready to leap out of the top windows.

Penny went quite pale, 'I don't think I could learn to do that,' she said.

'Your only hope of getting in is to pretend to be a cook,' I reminded her.

The flats behind were not imposing at all; they were just ordinary LCC blocks, some of which were being used as extra offices, while the upstairs ones were used as billets. Somebody showed us the right door to knock on, and there we were in an office which was only imposing because it was obviously efficiently run, talking to a very nice young woman, who wasn't after all so terribly grand, and didn't seem to mind a bit telling us all about the work.

Every now and then the telephone on her desk tinkled, and she'd press a buzzer and a firewoman would rush in, stand to attention, and produce folders called Weekly Return of Woman Power.

... folders called Weekly Return of Woman Power.

'Can you tell us,' said Penny, 'exactly what would happen to us if we did join?'

'Well, you'd have to get an ED60 – you know about that? And take it to a station where they recruit, and you'd have your interview and be told the hours. Forty-eight on, you know. Twenty-four off. The forty-eight on is partly stand-by, in fact, very largely, and partly duty periods.'

'Can you sleep in the stand-by time?'

'Obviously. You're expected to.'

'Er – what on?' I asked.

'It depends; generally we have stretchers or wooden platforms – you'd never believe how comfy they can be with a good mattress. You're allowed three blankets.'

'Just like our shelter bunks,' I reminded Penny, who was looking depressed. She does hanker for box springs.

'You soon get used to it,' said the officer. 'The duty periods vary – you may be on from ten till five, or five to eleven, or eleven at night to seven next morning. When you're standing by, you can usually get short leave for shopping, so you aren't completely cut off. And your twenty-four hours comes round very quickly.'

'And pay?' I put in.

'The usual ARP rate for firewomen.'

'But is there absolutely nothing to do when you've got through your eight hours on duty?' said Penny. 'That might be dull …'

'Oh, there're plenty of odd jobs …'

'Charring?' I asked.

'Well, you can't avoid it altogether, can you? There are the sleeping quarters to tidy and so on. But unless you're a cook, you get your food without having to worry over it. We mess in canteens usually; sometimes the girls bring their own plates and cutlery. That's to avoid those awful washing-up fatigues. But of course arrangements vary from Station to Station.'

'Can we choose what we want to be? Do we get posted to a Station straight away, and have we any say about where it is?'

'Well, you've got a training course first. Everyone has to take that; you live at home and attend by the day. It gives you a chance to see how you'll really like the work, and us a chance to see if you're suited to it. We only want people who are really keen.'

We wanted to know what we'd have to learn and where we'd have to go.

'Training centres in most areas,' said our officer. 'You get taught Brigade organisation, Communications, Keeping of Records, log-books and so on, Then there's an ARP course – high explosives, gas, incendiaries, stirrup pump drill. And Squad Drill and PT.'

'Not jumping out of windows?' asked Penny.

'We don't need athletes, except perhaps for despatch riding. We're just beginning to use girls for that. If you've got plenty of nerve and thrive on excitement, you enjoy it. I wouldn't myself. People volunteer for that. Usually your job depends a bit on how you pass out of the training course; there's an exam – and we try to find out what people can do best ... they work so much better if they like what they're doing.'

'What would we be likely to have to do?' I asked. 'If we weren't too old for it, that is.'

'Oh, dear me, we take recruits up to fifty for all departments, and over when they're cooks. You might be drivers, or if you were good shorthand typists or accountants, you'd go into the administrative section. Or you'd go into the Watch Room.'

'Is Administrative just ordinary clerking when you get down to it?' I asked.

'It's interesting – and it's needed. You can see for yourselves that an organisation this size simply can't be run without a lot of paper work – the pay department alone is pretty vast. It was nearly all done by men. But now the girls take over and release the fit men for fire-fighting – or for the Services. So even if the work isn't actually exciting, you can always feel you're doing a thoroughly good job because you're setting a man free for something stiffer. And there's plenty of work to keep you busy.'

'But I want to be a *driver*,' pleaded Penny. 'Don't you want drivers?'

They did want drivers; they were even prepared to teach likely people; but the standard was high. No, the girls did not drive fire engines. Or pumps. They had plenty to do driving staff cars, canteens and light vans for petrol.

'In the blitz, too?' Penny asked.

'Specially in the blitz. If things are bad, our canteens are sometimes kept hard at it. So're the cars. And right in the hottest parts each time. Our drivers have seen enough thrills in the blitz to last them a life-time.'

'And what's the Watch Room?' I asked.

'Now I think that's the most interesting job of all. Probably that's because I began there myself. Really, it's fascinating. You're right at the nerve centre of everything; all incoming and outgoing messages pass through, and that's where all the pumps are mobilised.'

'I can see that would be exciting,' I said. 'Do your girls really do a lot of that?'

'Goodness me, most Watch Rooms are largely staffed by girls. Specially at the small Stations. At the bigger ones, they work for a man. But even so, it is really responsible work; you've got to get the right type of girl and she's got to be thoroughly trained. You see, the very newest rabbit might have to order out the pumps.'

'You mean, she might be left on her own to take decisions?'

'She certainly might. If she were posted to a small Station, there might be only three girls on Watch Room duties – one would be away on leave, one standing by, one on duty. So you see, your rabbit might be on duty by herself when a call came in.'

'And would she know what to do?'

'She wouldn't be there long if she didn't ... She's got to be level-headed and quick-witted, for even in a lull, or a very moderate raid, there might be a fire for which all that Station would be out – the officer in charge too. She'd be alone, except for the girl standing by. Of course she has a direct line connecting her with the Station immediately above her, but they won't thank her for pestering them.'

We nodded; you could see that here was a job that really mattered, something you could feel glad to be allowed to do.

'And if there's a blitz,' the officer went on persuasively, 'those two girls have got to keep that telephone manned, that Watch Room going whatever happens. Well – I don't need to tell you how they've done it. You've only got to read your papers to know that.'

We had seen the papers; but we hadn't really thought what it would feel like to be almost alone in a Watch Room, keeping the phone going as long as there was a phone to keep going, knowing that however bad things got, you couldn't get up and go. That took nerve all right, a different sort of nerve from the kind that sees you through a night of blitz when you're out on the job. But nerve.

'Any more questions? You must have lots … promotion, now …'

'Can anyone get promotion?' Penny asked.

'You have to serve six months in the ranks. The first step up is Leading Firewoman – one red stripe. She's in charge of a watch of girls – that may only be half a dozen. Next, Assistant Group Officer – she has charge of about fifty women. Two red stripes. Then there's Group Officer – that's a staff appointment – she has three red stripes and she probably has charge of a group of Stations. And then there's Assistant Area Officer, with one silver stripe. So you see, there's plenty of scope for ability to rise – specially with the way the Fire Service is expanding and being reorganised.' (It wasn't till later that year that the AFS became the National Fire Service.) 'And we want our girls to get on. There's the Staff College down at Brighton, you know. Eventually all officers will pass through that. Does this help you at all?'

Penny said she still only wanted to be a driver, but I agreed that work in a Watch Room would probably be far more interesting really.

'I'll take you to see ours. Of course, this being headquarters, it's the brain of the whole concern here in London. We have a minimum of seventeen girls on duty in a raid; there's always a man Mobilising Officer and one senior woman officer.'

They practically clicked their heels.

Outside, firewomen were running up and down the stairs, they saluted; when our officer spoke to them, they said Yes Madam and No Madam and practically clicked their heels.

'They make us look a Bolshie lot,' Penny whispered. 'But I like it. You know how I adore efficiency.'

Firewomen in trousers were scrumming round a door called Despatch Riders; firewomen in skirts and horn rims were to-ing and fro-ing from the rabbit warren of offices; firewomen in overcoats and forage caps were going out on short leave.

In the Watch Room itself, so carefully planned, so well air-conditioned, so unobtrusively lighted, it was very quiet except for the babble round the switchboard where about half a dozen girls on high stools, head-phones clipped to their curls, dealt with incoming and outgoing calls on a miniature exchange. That, it seemed, was a skilled job, though recruits could learn it without previous experience. Sometimes they went out to a GPO course and specialised in switchboard work.

Behind them was a row of booths, at which, in raids, other girls received the calls as these were sorted out at the switchboard; they wrote out the messages and handed them to girl runners who took them across to the officer in charge.

'This is a very slack time, there's nothing to do,' said our officer, 'so you can't really imagine what a hive it is when we're busy. These boards now …' She took us over to a series of boards, studded with coloured discs, and nearby, a large-scale map. 'We have two or three girls working on each of these,' she said. The main board had a disc for every pump, another had discs for every special appliance available in the whole area. The state of parties for the whole of inner London could be seen at a glance, for as the pumps and appliances went out, so the discs were moved. On the map, every fire was plotted and the position of every pump, the allocation of all special appliances, could be marked.

'Of course I simply couldn't bear to be anywhere but in the Watch Room at headquarters,' I said. 'And working on those boards.'

Our officer laughed. 'It's skilled work,' she said. 'But you see, there's not so very much of the stand-by service about us. Even without raids, we can undertake to keep our people busy, and there's so much to learn and so much scope for common sense that our people simply don't get bored.'

As we left the Watch Room, a pretty young woman passed and saluted. She wore a medal ribbon. Penny asked about her with awe.

She'd been decorated a little time ago, after a very bad night, when she'd worked at three Stations, moving on to each as the last was bombed. At the third, there was trouble, and when all the pumps were out, a fire started. She had the foresight to get her girls out safely and the pluck to lead them.

Penny turned to look after her: then she took a deep breath and said if she could get an ED60, could she volunteer at once and I would too?

'We shall be very glad to see you,' said our officer. But she didn't sound as if she thought she ever would.

All the way home, Penny said she didn't mind a bit about scarcely ever being at home and always sleeping on stretchers because she wanted to work for a Service where there was plenty to do. 'I'd sleep on the floor, Mildred, you know I would – I'd stand out in the rain under a lamp-post if it would help the war,' she said. 'Think how we should enjoy interesting work, responsible work, exacting work. That's what we want, Mildred. I know we aren't as young as most of those kids, but let's do something worth doing, let's live hard, let's run a few risks, while we still can.'

But when we got to the Station next day, Greeny was standing by the notice board looking sour, and there was a Service Order informing us that we couldn't be released from the Ambulance Service for any other work after the day before yesterday.

Penny went bright pink; she took off her cap and threw it on the ground and danced on it.

'Damn it,' she said, 'I'll never get an ED60 now.'

XIV April, 1941

It was early April; the street corners were alight with barrow loads of daffodils, and in the gardens of bombed houses, almond blossom and forsythia smiled at the sun.

We sat by the window of Penny's sitting-room in the warm twilight, Penny and Belinda and I. Barky was there too for, with the lull, she had emerged from her work in the East End; we darned and we knitted and we brooded, while Penny moved restlessly from the wireless to the electric fire, switching them on and off alternately.

Belinda yawned, pushed back her curls and stretched out her long legs, prodding her heels into the carpet as she considered her grey uniform skirt, splashed with tea and stained with mud which hadn't brushed off properly.

'Hell, what a mess one looks in the spring,' she said. 'I'm sick of looking a mess, and I'm sick of driving tea-urns about. People can't really *need* so much tea now.'

'I'm completely and utterly fed up,' said Penny. 'I didn't even mind doing nothing in the Ambulance when I hadn't got to, but now I've *got to* by law, it makes me quite sick.'

'Everybody's feeling pretty much the same. I daresay even Barky's fed up,' I said, looking across at Barky, sitting very straight in Penny's low Hepplewhite chair, knitting needles clacking in and out of soft white wool for a baby's vest. She looked at me over the tops of her spectacles; her face crumpled into a smile.

'Not at all,' she said. 'It's a treat to me to have a few evenings to myself.'

'Even the East End doesn't need you so much now,' I said, 'when the emergency's just about over.'

'When people are very poor,' she said dryly, 'they live on the edge of emergencies.'

'Oh dear,' said Penny, looking quickly and guiltily at her nice room, whose solid comfort had survived the blitz.

'Soup kitchens and girls' clubs and Scouts and mothers' meetings,' Belinda pouted. 'But they aren't so exciting as war emergencies.'

Miss Barker's grey topknot quivered.

'For us,' she said, 'there's always a war on – war against misery and dirt and ignorance and unbelief. This war only makes it worse, that's all.'

Penny said, 'Oh dear,' again, and Belinda said crossly, 'But don't you *ever* feel a little flat?'

'I haven't got time,' said Miss Barker. ' And in my opinion, you people spend a great deal too much time measuring how bored you are. You would have a better sense of proportion if you came and looked at the East End.'

We said, 'Yes' meekly, and I promised to go. Penny can't bear to be harrowed because she has a very soft heart, so in the end, I went by myself, lurching down in a bus that twisted in and out between old craters, and wherever the devastation was worst, there the flower sellers had set their barrows, till the smell of ruin was daunted by the smell of spring.

A girl conductor, who had been frowning over arithmetic, leaning against the steps as if her legs were tired, came for my fare. She wasn't rightly sure where I ought to get off.

But a little dark sparrow of a woman, in a battered feather toque, was instantly and indignantly sure. She leaned across to tell me I wanted the King's 'Ead and it wasn't more than fivepence.

'Comin' to see the sights?' she said presently. 'Well – see that ole mess-up over there? I was in that, believe me or believe me not, the night it went.'

I murmured admiring wonder.

'Well, when I say in it – it was me chest saved me. We'd been bombed down our way, see? Sitting in the kitchen I was an' looked up to see the blinkin' wall leaning over me. Only sittin' right under it, like, I didn't get a scratch. Wot's more, there wasn't even a plate broke in me scullery. Of course, upstairs was a bit of rough and tumble. So I came up West, to see me sister. And I 'adn't been up more'n a day before I got caught in one of these raids, and I went down in that place, back there. Big jeweller's shop it was … shelter for fifty, it says. An' wen I got in, the warden chap down there, he sez, "You're in luck, Mother. There's forty-nine of us down 'ere, so you're the last as can come in."'

She took a deep breath. 'Well, I sits there a bit. Only, see dear, it's stuffy in a place like that. And I'm troubled with me chest. Asthma, see. So by an' by I sez to meself, well it's no use stoppin' 'ere to choke – weezin' away like a' 'ole engine I was. So up I gets to go, and the warden – ever such a good lookin' young chap 'e was – he come with me to see me out. And when we got out in the street, we falls slap on our faces, 'earin' something comin' down, you see. And wen we gets up, the warden takes one look be'ind 'im and 'e sez, "Thank God for your asthma, Mother." Yes, there was forty-eight of em trapped there. It was me chest saved me. Or Providence.'

'Pretty marvellous,' I said.

She tossed her head till the feather toque rustled. 'I didn't stop up West after that. Didn't seem worth it. Trust Providence, I sez to meself, trust Providence, me girl and go back 'ome. So back I went; we got some boards, me ole man an' me, and we blocked up the 'ole in our wall and I 'ung up a red baize tablecloth I'd got no use for. Looked right down comic, our room did. You 'ad to laugh …'

She was laughing now at the thought of it, till her face creased up into a hundred little wrinkles.

'A real scream, it was. But mind you, it makes me fair mad to see our 'omes knocked about like that. If I was ten years younger, I'd be in munitions. But me legs is bad too, see? So I just 'ave to make do shopping for the married girls in our street that's gone in the factories. Seven lots of rations I gets each week … an' if I do 'ave to 'ang about a bit, gettin' 'em the best of everythink, I jes' works out in me mind 'ow many bullets them girls'll be turning out in the time I saves 'em … That's your stop, dearie. Where the King's 'Ead was.'

Demolition men were clearing the remains of the King's Head from the pavement as I turned down the narrow street that led off the main road. It was desolate, unkempt, that row of blind-eyed houses, the roofs patched with felting, the windows boarded up. At first you were sure that nobody lived there, and then you noticed that sometimes the boarded windows were open at the top, to admit air, if not light. And sometimes a patch of cellophane had been let into the woodwork, and showed the fringe of a curtain, the frond of a fern set there to catch the sun. Our West End houses had had surgical treatment; the hopeless cases were cleared away and the habitable ones restored almost to normal. But these streets had just had a dose of first-aid, made rent-producing, and then abandoned.

They squatted there, these ugly little houses, blinded and battered, obstinately waiting for their tenants, working now in shops or factories, railways or docks, who would obstinately return to their overcrowded dingy rooms and obstinately insist on making them into a home.

Three little houses made the settlement Barky had sent me to see; they were exactly the same as the others, only sprucer. And outside one window, there was a kind of greenhouse which held a display of pictures, a reproduction of Raphael's 'Madonna', another of a 'Knight at Prayer', a watercolour of trees and a lake, a group of fairies, and a row of little wooden animals. I found myself rubbing my nose against the glass in company with two small boys who breathed heavily and then smeared the mist away with grimy hands.

The guardian angel of the place was a crisp, white-haired little woman, simmering with energy like a kettle coming to the boil. She took me upstairs to her study where books and papers were stacked beside her chair, and every inch of the walls was covered with pictures, or photographs or framed quotations, rhyme sheets and mottoes and solemn thoughts and calendars. It was a queer little museum, where the exhibits were chosen for the happiness they had brought.

As I looked round me, she laughed.

'D'you think the only thing we can do for the poor is to share our bread and cheese and coal with them?' she asked. 'Because I assure you, it's much more important to share ideas.'

'That's why you have pictures outside as well as in?'

She nodded, 'People stop to look – and when they come in it all makes for a chat.'

Suddenly you saw how that small room had hummed with the talk of generations of mothers and children, how the little girls who had heard the musical box with wonder had grown into the leggy creatures who star-gazed at the fairy pictures, and how, years later, their babies listened to the musical box in their turn.

'And they still love your pictures – even in these days?'

'Dear me, yes. This blitz, it's a phase that passes. The war's a phase. It'll come to its end. But the work goes on.'

She gave me tea and talked about the work, and how the settlement had grown up round the school, because through the school, you got to know every family in the place.

'Of course we're not denominational,' she remarked. 'I don't care for competition in religion. I don't like to hear a churchwoman say, "Well I 'ad to go to Chapel to get little Tom 'is boots."'

And now, though so many children had been sent away, there was still plenty to do. Just ordinary everyday jobs: comforting people in trouble, caring for people who were homeless, clothing people who had lost everything, there was nothing new in all that.

I supposed that perhaps it was really only new to people like us, who'd never cared very much what happened to our neighbours.

'Oh, I daresay in the West End you're surprised if people you haven't been introduced to behave like decent human beings if a raid comes along. But you see, the poor have always been good neighbours to one another … that's something the West End can learn from us. The most surprising people are good to one another – I shall never forget seeing two smart girls stopping to carry an old granny's bundles. Why, if I was bombed to-night, I can think of a dozen who would take me in …'

The little houses must seem very frail in a raid, I thought.

'Naturally, we've had some very disagreeable nights … but just about here, we've been lucky. An incendiary did come through

Two girls picked up her bundles.

the roof one night, but a very kind man most obligingly put it out.'

After we'd had tea I saw over the place, which seemed to be propped up on pyramids of parcels. Apparently all the gifts of clothes and toys and books and pictures and oddments that were given to the settlement ultimately turned into Bundles; Farthing Bundles for Children, Penny Bundles for Grown-ups, Christmas Bundles and Birthday Bundles, and what was left filled a room full of coats and dresses and suits and trifles that were sold cheaply once a week.

You forgot the blitz, you forgot the war, as you listened to the stories that went with the Bundles, but as we went through to look at the garden, we passed a small back room, dark because the window had been blocked up and the piles of parcels reinforced with pit-props. Between them was a table, stacked high with Christmas cards, Valentines, Easter cards, birthday cards and postcards, and beside the table was a long box nearly partitioned into compartments labelled Christmas, Birthday, Mother, Baby, Pretty, Comic, Devotional – High and Low.

On the disagreeable nights, the guardian angel liked to sit there, sorting out the cards into their categories so that they could give pleasure again, earmarking those she thought specially appropriate; you could see her, spectacles perched on her nose, flipping them over, chuckling now and then to herself as she considered the niceties of High and Low Easter cards to the tune of bombers overhead.

Down by the docks I went next; and in a sector where oil wharves and timber wharves had blazed, lined by dismal, gutted warehouses, a steamer suddenly peered at me over a row of chimney pots, and I looked down from the top deck of a bus and saw little grey tramps berthed alongside piers that might have come straight out of a W W Jacobs' story. And here, where the destruction at some points seemed so merciless that you wondered how any set of human beings could have survived such an inferno and kept their reason, you came suddenly on pin-new unblemished blocks of flats, gardens that flowered happily, rows of smoke-blackened cottages and a shabby Settlement House by a garden where cheerful young women were teaching youthful matrons how to skip decoratively for health.

'D'you mean to say you still do this sort of thing?' I asked, as a matron tangled her feet in the skipping rope to the giggles of the class.

'We like to keep things going as much as we can,' the warden said. 'Of course, if there was a bad raid to-night, well, this kind of party would just drop out for the time being. We'd be a Third Line Rest Centre and probably we'd have to turn to and feed several hundred people. Not to mention fitting them out with clothes – supplied by WVS, you know. And running the Citizens' Advice Bureau.'

'You mean you can just switch over from everyday things to blitz things?'

'But they aren't all that different. Of course you can't have clubs and outings so much if there are lots of raids, but that's a detail. If we aren't looking after people here, we're looking after them in shelters – but they're the same people – you just change your way of working, that's all.'

'You've got it all taped now, I can see that. But, at first ...?'

Ah, at first ... At first, at the very first, they'd gone out to watch the dog-fights over the Thames, excited, elated, not knowing the horrors of bomb-shattered nights. And then the fires had come; and they had gone out to supervise shelters and steady the shelterers, to improvise kitchens, when gas, electricity and water had gone off, and the roads out were blocked.

'The thing I remember most about the first night is dashing backwards and forwards from the shelter (in those days, shelters had nothing much in them but benches and people) to heat up babies' bottles in our house. Babies won't wait, whatever's dropping, and really their screams were worse than the bombs.'

Somehow, from old stores and new stores hastily collected a clothing depot was opened; somehow, though there was no kitchen big enough to cook for the hungry hundreds, a communal feeding centre was improvised. They turned old sheds into dining-rooms, they roped in all the people who still had stoves to help.

'I remember coming back at dinner time one day, to find my assistant simply frantic: she kept saying, "I can't think what I've done with my other leg." There were joints and vegetables and puddings in other people's ovens, all up and down the road.'

'You had fun?'

'Of course we had fun: if it hadn't been for all the awful suffering, we'd have enjoyed it. Always doing just a bit more than you can, it's a grand feeling ... you understand what makes people go off and explore or climb mountains or fly the Atlantic.'

They were young, the people there. Very young, some of them. Just kids taking a course in social science, the sort of nice kids you wanted to send away to some remote quiet place to put into safe keeping for the peace that is to come. But they didn't see it that way; it wasn't that they wanted excitement, it was just that they were on a job and they happened to be in love with the job and wouldn't let it go.

At one Centre where, before the war, a whole network of Boys' and Girls' Clubs had flourished, the very youngsters who had come every peace-time night to play and act and dance, came every siren night, after their long day's work, to do another job. They set to and cut sandwiches and made tea and cocoa, and then went out, dodging shrapnel, incendiaries and high explosives without even the comfort of a tin hat, to get that food and drink round to the hungry, weary people sheltering in cellars.

'Sixty gallons of cocoa,' the secretary said. 'Yes, sometimes we'd serve all of that in a night.'

Sixty gallons of cocoa, I thought, carried through streets where almost every raid must have brought new devastation, by kids who were too young for the Forces, but not too young to face horror and risk their lives just so that hungry people might be fed.

'It's rather horrid, sometimes,' said the secretary, 'if raids are bad, and I get in first; not nice, waiting for the other parties to come back, waiting and wondering, wondering whether perhaps this time you shouldn't have let them go. But they've always come through all right.'

And of course, the place had been a Third Line Rest Centre too, and busy most nights. Of course they'd sponsored emergency feeding, of course they had a clothes store and sometimes they had reclothed more than two hundred people in a week. All sorts of people, friends and strangers, had turned up to help. In the daytime, they'd started a play centre for the children who hadn't been evacuated; they'd opened their doors to any wandering children, brought them in and fed them and taught them and made them happy. As you listened, looking round the bright rooms, with their equipment for gym and games, their stage and piano, you could see that somehow they had carried all the friendly gaiety and zest of peace-time into the blitz, and out again.

And at the other end of the scale, you'd come across little communities of devoted workers who'd almost snap at you, across desks piled high with official forms and case sheets and appeals: 'I've been here for forty years; d'you think I'd leave now?'

Comparative youngsters in the fifties and sixties tagged a warden's job on to their work, doing their nightly patrols in flame-lit streets.

'We're lucky,' one of them said, opening large, childlike blue eyes very wide indeed, 'the men usually make us take the beat near the best shelter in the place – even if you never go in it's nice to know it's there.'

One night, a bread basket had spilled incendiaries up and down the road, and in her hurry to swat one of them, she had tripped and gone sprawling. Shriller than the whistles of bombs came a ribald laugh, and a small boy danced towards her.

'Coo, miss, I seen you a chasin' them incendiaries; come on and I'll give you a 'and.'

The ruined warehouses and damaged blocks of flats fairly shouted their dramatic story, but you couldn't get anyone to tell it; but you heard of nights when droves of people, too shaken to tramp to the official rest centres, had sheltered in the Settlement. 'Of course the warden'll take us in,' they said and came, carrying children and cats and radios, gramophones, dogs and budgerigars, until the order had gone out: 'Birds and animals in the coal hole, please.'

"Birds and animals in the coal hole ..."

You met District Nurses, too, who had gone about their day's work, cycling down flooded streets and scrambling over ruins to get to their patients.

'Well, I was blown off my cycle once,' said one of them, a wide-eyed young woman with a curly smile. 'It was quite a pleasant experience; a current of warm air just lifted me off the bike, and there I was, sitting beside it in the road.'

Wherever you went, stories of miraculous escapes counterbalanced stories of human woe that seemed past bearing.

'There's seven in our family gone,' one pallid young woman said to me, as I stopped to look at a ruin. 'All took when this place went, the night before they was to be evacuated …'

'Lookin' at our wide open spaces?' said another cheerfully in a place where a whole network of houses had just been wiped flat. 'Get plenty of fresh air now, don't we? Fancy, there was only two hurt the night that ole street come down.'

A great mission settlement had colonised that district, setting about the job of saving souls and lives with an efficient drive that seemed more typical of commerce than of social work.

'We like to think we're one jump ahead of the authorities all the time,' said the young minister in charge, 'we reckoned that there were three big problems: shelter-health – no one had imagined that people would have to live in shelters; shelter feeding – emergency cooking nearly always followed the need for it; shelter boredom. So we just tackled them. We had the premises, we had the staff, we had the equipment.'

They had their own excellent shelter, better equipped than most from the start; the sick bay was run by a girl of nineteen … 'Got sick of standing by in the West End and came to us … she's done a pretty tough job of work too. We run a regular service, touring all the shelters in our district every night, with a capable nurse who can spot illness. We've got our own ambulances now, so that we can pack invalids right off to hospital before an epidemic can get going.' He marched me round to see the shelter and the centre of all blitz activities, where men and women had seen what should be done and what had been a plan at dawn had become a working reality by dusk. 'Every morning one of us'd take a car and do the damage – visit every incident and bring the homeless in.'

'This business of feeding,' he went on briskly, 'we've got our own mobile canteens now ... we drive round the shelters with food and drink – early breakfasts for people going to work – that sort of thing ... of course we've our own canteen too.' I admired it, I admired the shelter and the sick bay, where the nineteen-year-old, who looked far too pretty to be tough, was checking stores, her face quite unshadowed by anything she'd seen.

'This question of boredom; nothing worse for morale than having people cooped up night after night and day after day with nothing to do. We soon got on to that – our concert parties toured the shelters, and of course, up here, we had our own shelterers' club – gave 'em the use of a big room, darts, billiards, piano and so on. Interesting the way community life grew up at once.'

Upstairs we pounded to the great green painted club room, with gay coloured tables and wicker chairs and books and magazines. 'See that enclosure over there? We set up an inquiry bureau – disentangled all the regulations, contacted all the authorities, got people fixed up double quick with forms for claiming compensation, railway vouchers and country billets and all that.'

'It must have been a tremendous job ...'

'It only wanted *organising* ...' In a little office, he produced a folder full of statistics, graphs showing progress, so that in a moment he could tell you the exact state of every activity, the number of concerts given, the number of cups of tea served.

But just the same, all this was a side line; the real work of saving souls went on blitz or no blitz. He ran me quickly up the street so that we should be just in time to see an afternoon service, and hear eight hundred mothers singing hymns.

After that I tracked down Barky and begged a cup of tea. She was one of the people who didn't much like working in gangs, the ones who lived by themselves in a slum house, in a slum street, helping to bear the burdens of a whole parish, or doing the School Care Committee work that was still so sorely needed.

'Care Committee work,' said Barky, as I sagged into her one armchair, in her little front room, whose windows had long since lost their glass, 'isn't what it was. So many schools closed, and so many fiddly, tiresome jobs, getting clothes for evacuated children. But still, I have a little leisure, specially now I don't do so much in the shelters.'

She'd volunteered very early on, as a Shelter Marshal.

'I never was fond of tunnels, either,' she said. 'And the first place I had was a tunnel. It smelt of trains for the first six hours, and – hm – of humanity and lack of drains for the next. Still, you didn't hear much there – you could get some sleep.'

'But what did you do with them, all those people, cooped up there?'

'We couldn't do much at first. The children were a little pathetic, so I got a young friend of mine to come along and help. She used to come just after dusk, with a roll of brown paper and a lot of chalks. I can see her now, coming in, rain dripping off her mackintosh; and all the children, peering out from behind their mothers, squeals stopping in mid-howl, and they used to run off, tripping over all the bedding and fall into line behind her, following her around the place as if she were the Pied Piper. A curious sight it was, to see them settle down to watch her draw and

Followed her as if she were the Pied Piper.

then pick up the chalks themselves, their little tongues hanging out, crouching under the hurricane lamps, working away as if nothing mattered in the world but the pretty pictures.'

I asked if things got easier when bunks and proper lights and lavatories and First Aid Posts arrived.

'The place was hit before we got those,' she said dryly and added, with a sigh, 'I was off duty.'

'Believe me,' she said after a moment, 'it's not the danger that hurts, nor the discomfort. It's the sorrow. Trying to trace broken families … to find some little thing you can say or do … and you can't. Have another cup of tea?'

'Don't think,' she said, as she poured it out, 'that it's only the winners of the George Medal who've beaten the enemy. It's all the millions of ordinary people who've got on with their jobs. You young women in Civil Defence, you think if you aren't doing something exciting you're no use. Get over that idea. Wars aren't run by rising to emergencies, but by plodding along so steadily that when the emergency comes you don't have far to rise to it.'

As she took me to the bus, we passed a tall white-haired man, in the flapping black habit of a priest; his quiet face had that look of remote happiness that always makes one wonder.

'Good night, Father.'

'Good night, my dear child.'

'He'll be going to see someone who's sick,' she said. 'He'd go just the same whether there was a raid or not. It wouldn't make any difference – except that if it were very bad he'd probably sit up all night with someone too ill to be moved.'

'I see,' I said. 'Yes, I see.'

That, then, was why all these people, living and working among the poor, were really the shock troops of Civil Defence, even though they never wore a uniform or gave the matter a thought. It was because, after years of service, people knew that they were utterly reliable, that always they would do the job, the very simplest humble job, just the same whether there was a raid or not, because they loved the people and the place and the work more than they loved their lives or their health or their nerves. They tagged Civil Defence work on to their other job, but by far the biggest contribution they made was just being themselves, being the sort of people to whom a whole neighbourhood could turn and say, 'Whatever 'appens, you ain't going to pack up an' leave us.'

XV Spring Blitz

Penny and I had eight hours' leave; we took the car and went into the country, and lay flat on our backs underneath a chestnut tree that held out sticky china hands to the sun. The bank was stippled with primroses, the warm wind tasted of blossom, and in the fields ridiculous lambs staggered about among cowslips.

We lay there drowsily happy. All the springs we'd ever known, when our husbands were young and the children were tiny and you could still hope all things, seemed to be threaded together like a dream daisy chain. Fragile as the real chain over which my fingers fumbled, if you moved, it would snap.

A young bee buzzed inquisitively over Penny's face, and she sat up.

'Oh dear,' she said, 'it's so lovely I almost think I'd enjoy a good cry.'

'You haven't time,' I said, dropping my daisies into the grass. 'A good cry takes quite two hours and we're on duty at five.'

'Up the second half of the night for certain,' said Penny, her tearful happiness turning a little sour. 'Getting up at two-thirty and shivering till seven – and nothing ever happens.'

Things happened that night. It wasn't even decently dark before the wireless faded, the siren howled and the guns cracked.

'Just passing over,' Mark said, scarcely lifting her head from her darning.

'Dropping in, believe you me,' said the man on patrol, a small round Irishman whose boots always looked too big for him. 'Come'n see the flares.'

Penny and I had nothing to worry about; we were only fourth out so we strode casually towards the door. Penny whispered:

'Do your knees feel funny too, Gibsy?'

'No, but my stomach does.'

'Oh dear, we're shockingly out of practice.'

Outside the silver night was rainbow coloured: as we watched, flare after flare dropped lazily down, like decorations on a giant's Christmas tree. Away to the right of us petals of flame blossomed already beyond the jagged line of roofs. Almost immediately the clamour of fire engines daunted the guns, and as the engines surged down the street I wondered how many girls were left alone to man the Stations' Watch Rooms. Down at Lambeth they would be busy now, and already the girls at the switchboards would be peppered with calls, and as the pumps were mobilised, the little discs on the great record boards would move in and out, and on the maps the girls would be marking the site of that very fire and showing the position of the pumps called to it. Every Watch Room in London would be on the alert, each a little ganglion in the nerve system of the Fire Service, manned by women trained for this very night, keyed up to this very emergency. Did any of them for one grim second wonder if their Watch Room would be there at dawn?

'Whoopee!' said the man on patrol, as a crack louder than thunder split the sky.

Away to the south a pillar of flame climbed up the night, then turned to a pillar of smoke, red in the glow of the fires beneath, silver rimmed in the light of the moon above.

'Come in at once, please Penny, and you too Gibsy,' the ASO came purposefully towards us. 'It is not a firework display. One bit of shrapnel and we are an ambulance short.'

It was stuffy inside. Bilson had huddled herself in the corner with a crossword. Greeny was stitching veiling on to a flowered toque. Mark was still darning. The men's leader was playing patience. I took five soda mints as the telephone rang. Report and Control wanted to check our state of parties.

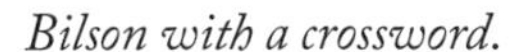

Bilson with a crossword.

'I said six ambulances, not seven. Six ambulances, four cars, eighteen personnel,' said the shift-leader. 'Tchah, they've got a beginner on the line.'

Poor thing, I thought, swallowing a soda mint, wondering if in the bowels of Report and Control some unhappy female were meeting her first raid, sticky with nervousness as she struggled to hear the hurried voices coming over the wire as some warden in a sandbagged post phoned in the XYZ that would set the services moving. And then in the inner Control Room as the messages came through, each call for help would change into an incident number, marked on a board and the rescue parties, stretcher parties and ambulances would become little counters in an official game. Already the plotters would have begun to mark the damage on the big maps, and surely by now there should be an outgoing message for us?

'You'd think,' said Mark, looking up as though she'd heard me, 'that they'd have had us out before this with all these fires.'

The building jarred; it lurched upwards then sank into its socket like an obstinate tooth. The card table skidded, and a tin hat clanked to the floor.

Bilson said, 'How sardines do repeat! We've had sardines twice running for supper, and they always give me a bad night.'

The building shook itself again. The lights swung backwards and forwards before they flickered out. The telephone began to ring as we got the hurricane lamps going. It went on ringing quite steadily till in ten minutes every ambulance was out. Penny and I trotted clumsily across the yard; the old Ford was chugging over crossly as we got in. I rasped the gears very badly, but nobody heard.

We hadn't been so close to a fire before, and we didn't like it much, but two of our ambulances were waiting there already. I parked behind them and Penny and I both got out and walked a little way up the road. In front of us, crumpled into a hole in the ground, was something that had once been a fire engine. We must have heard it clanging down the street; we must have watched the crew polishing the brass many a morning as we came to work.

'*Oh*,' cried Penny, 'it'll be one of our own – from our Station.' A staff fire service car drove up very fast. The girl driver backed it into a side turning as an officer got out. Another fire engine came along; another crew got to work on the flames, and above us we could hear a plane running up to the target before he released his bombs. We turned back to our own ambulance again, and a warden came out of the glow towards us.

'You that third ambulance? Don't think we'll need you; still as you are here, you might clear some of this. Like to load up this poor fellow?' He shone his torch into the shadow. There was nothing the matter with the body except that it had no head. Penny began to say crossly that we couldn't carry corpses, when our own men's leader came up and bustled us off. We heard him giving the warden a raspberry in a voice shrill with distaste. In the end we took one dazed and shaken old man with a cut foot to a First Aid Post.

We were hardly back at the station before we were out again. There was another fire going close behind us, where a goods yard was burning like a gigantic Christmas pudding.

'What a waste of good whisky,' said Penny sadly. 'Come on: know your way? Go left at the gate as usual.'

I nodded, but as I pulled the wheel over, I heard another voice inside me saying, 'Turn right; turn *right*.' I swung the ambulance clumsily round, jarring the near-side tyre against the opposite kerb. Something came past us with a small sigh; we scarcely heard the crashing impact, but the road trembled till the ambulance bounced like a dud tennis ball.

'S-S-s-something missed us,' Penny said.

'Can you see if the Station's there?'

'Yes, the Station's there.'

We turned into the main road, flooded with golden light, hot as a tropical sun. Suddenly Penny began to chant, 'Thou shalt not be afraid for the terror by night, nor for the arrow that flieth by day; nor for the pestilence that walketh in darkness …'

I fumbled for the words, 'Nor for the destruction that wasteth at noontide … A thousand shall fall by thy side …'

'*Quite* a thousand, I should think,' Penny put in.

'And ten thousand at thy right hand, but it shall not come near thee ...'

'Nigh,' said Penny, 'not "near", and I do wish you'd keep in time, Gibsy, even if you can't keep in tune. Here's the place.'

A very young warden left the shelter of the doorway to gape at us.

'You the ambulance? Oh, I say, your casualty's gone. Felt better and gone home. So sorry you've been troubled.'

Penny began to talk very fast, but I wasn't listening. Penny and the ambulance, the bark of the guns, the whine of bombs racketing down among the flames, they were all equally unreal. As far as I knew, something called Mildred Gibson was still driving an ambulance along that main road, but I myself seemed to hang somewhere above it, my mind expanding slowly, painfully, till it enfolded a million others.

I could almost see little Miss Pym, in her Warden's Post, telephoning urgent messages, her voice as quiet and precise as if she were teaching book-keeping, though the road outside was pitted with craters and her fellow wardens were quenching the flames from a burst gas main. And at the same moment I felt I could watch Elizabeth, with her squad, choking as the smoke caught her throat, crawling towards an old woman trapped in a burning room, and Belinda, loading up her van with urns and buns, then jolting along over hose-pipes and chunks of masonry, to dole out the cups of tea that meant to weary men not only a good drink, but the ability to work longer, harder, faster.

The river would be alight again, bombs crashing on to warehouses and piers, the little launch rocking up and down over the glittering water. The girls in the RES would be going ashore with a landing party, climbing like cats over the debris to reach men and women cut off between the river and the ruins, or standing by to care for the maimed and wounded brought to them from a bombed pier or a sinking ship.

Every Settlement I knew would be a refuge, sheltering old men and women and children and dogs and budgerigars, sending out workers to lead in the homeless, while boys and girls in slick smart clothes set out to carry gallons of tea and cocoa to the hungry. And the shelter nearby, underneath the chapel, would echo to the shrill children's voices singing 'Daisy …. Daisy …' and 'I love Sixpence …' All over London thousands of simple women would turn and befriend their neighbours, waiting quietly for the dawn that seemed as slow as the birth of the world in coming. There were so many of us, friends though strangers, working with a strength beyond our own, a courage beyond our own, lit with an indestructible spirit that was life everlasting.

'I'm not sure,' said Penny, getting stiffly out of the ambulance that I had somehow parked neatly in its place. 'I'm really not at all sure, whether I'm alive or dead.'

'Cheer up,' said Mark, 'if you're dead, I am too; come and have a cup of tea.'

Just before dawn we were called out again.

'Your bomb, Penny,' said the ASO, 'I'm glad it's missed us all, but it's made casualties.'

We turned left at the gate this time and drove to the terrace just behind the station on which our near miss had landed. The thin note of the All Clear went. In every hospital and settlement and shelter and home, men and women would let fear go from them with a sigh, turning again to the jobs that were waiting, and in that shelter near us, a group of weary children, so hoarse that their voices scarcely filled the room, would fall asleep … 'sometimes they sing all night …'

We switched off our lights at last in a cold grey dawn that showed the crumpled houses torn away from their fellows so that a staircase rose into space and you could see into a roofless upper room, where the pictures still hung above the mantelpiece, on which a book lay open, and a small gate-legged table still carried its vase of daffodils though one foot hovered in space.

There were trapped casualties. No one knew quite how many. The rescue squads were busy already, filling the little baskets with debris, trying to work a rope around the big beam that lay athwart the pile of masonry.

A white-hatted warden held up his hand:

'Quiet, everybody.'

A little further back a young woman sat by herself on a broken step, the doorway of her lost home framing the sky. She unbuttoned her jacket and put her baby to her breast.

Silence lay thick over the street. He clanged a spade against a mass of metal. 'Anybody there?'

No one could hope to hear the answer, but in spite of ourselves we pressed forward.

'Quiet … anybody there?'

Suddenly he stooped, his ear to the rubble. The leader of the rescue party joined him, eyes half closed, face strained with listening.

Suddenly there was a spurt of activity.

'They've *answered*!' Penny said.

A lorry backed up so that a small crane it carried could deal with the beam; spades and pick axes clashed as the leader began to tunnel; the baskets of rubble were passed down by an eager chain of hands; stretcher bearers, wardens, police, ambulance drivers, men and women, we took our places, straining at the baskets, unable every now and then to resist tearing at the rubble with bare hands.

'Easy.'

We stood back. Further down the street a little cluster of people hung about, baskets and suitcases and bags of this and that at their feet, looking almost as if they were going on some early morning excursion. One woman was talking … talking … No one else said anything at all. They just stood there and waited, like sheep waiting for the sheepdog to move them to a new fold. A little further back a young woman sat by herself on a broken step, the doorway of her lost home framing the sky. She unbuttoned her jacket and put her baby to her breast.

Presently, a girl in a fur coat and a siren suit came out from the unscathed house opposite carrying a great tray laden with cups of tea. We took them eagerly, our mouths dry and hot with dust.

'She must have used at least two weeks' rations,' Penny said, as she watched her go in and come out again with more.

Near us two women wardens were checking lists.

'Number five, they're OK. They got out by the kitchen window. Eight was empty. The trouble's six and seven.'

A rescue man came up, tipping his tin hat back and mopping his face. 'Little chap wiv ginger whiskers, that mean anything to you?'

'That's number six – is he all right?'

'He's 'anging ead down; 'e's all right, but 'e thinks 'e's done for.'

'Doctor?'

The call went round; almost immediately a tubby, elderly woman in a neat blast coat and skirt came up. The wardens spoke to her, and she went with

A girl in a fur coat and a siren suit … carrying a great tray laden with cups of tea.

the rescue man to his tunnel. She crawled in; then she stuck; you could see her rump pressed close against the opening, her feet scrabbling in the dust. One of the rescue men gave her a push.

Still the baskets of rubble passed from hand to hand; still pick and spade clamoured against the bricks. The mists thinned; now it was a blue and gold spring day. A little wind shook the branches of a chestnut tree and scattered the white dust from the leaves. And still the baskets of rubble passed from hand to hand; still pick and spade clamoured against the bricks. The street was empty, for the wardens had taken people away to rest centres. Penny and I sat down on the step of the ambulance. I found two pieces of chewing gum and we sat and chewed as stolidly as cows to silence the rumblings of our empty stomachs. It was nearly nine. We would be relieved by a new shift in ten minutes. Penny looked at me; I looked at Penny. She said:

'I don't care, I'm *not* going till they get Ginger Whiskers out.'

There were probably twenty or thirty people trapped in there. Our minds were too tired to think about them; we just sat where we were and hoped and prayed, and hoped and prayed, and hoped and prayed for Ginger Whiskers.

'Hey girls, show a leg; get your stretcher out.'

The noise of pick and spade had stopped, the rescue men leant on their shovels; the stretcher party were busy now. We stood by to help load as they brought out Ginger Whiskers.

XVI Christmas, 1941

Next morning, when I took a bus to do some shopping, an old lady in the seat behind me insisted on paying my fare, and when Penny went to buy fish, the man looked from her uniform to the piece he meant to give her and said, 'Not good enough for you, sister,' as he changed it for a fresher one. All over London, simple people did little things like that again for the wardens, the NFS, rescue men, stretcher bearers, and ambulance drivers.

'Some of our people must have been pretty terrific,' Penny said solemnly, and she looked down at her shabby coat as if she were proud of it.

When Robin said, next time we were on duty, 'Say, aren't you glad now that we didn't quit the Service?' we knew what she meant.

For somehow that night, just those few flame-torn hours, had made up for weeks of waiting; and we, who had been so disconsolate, so out of heart with ourselves, were contented and whole again. Even though nothing spectacular had been required of us personally, each of us could feel, somewhere inside ourselves, that when the people round us had been in for a tough time, we had at least been able to make things easier, and in the midst of crazy destruction, we had perhaps helped to save a life or two.

'I don't mind,' Penny said, 'if I never do anything again. Ever. I don't mind how long I sit here now.'

But when the lull seemed likely to be permanent, it wasn't really so easy. At first we were just content to be together: we weren't edgy or quarrelsome or jumpy, but placidly glad to be alive, and the greening, brilliant gardens, the soft nights and the gentle dawns had a poignancy that they had never held before.

As the moon rounded, so our pulses quickened, and without saying anything, we would check up on our equipment: when the nights darkened peaceably again, we would say:

'Well, I reckon we've got to be ready for much worse raids this autumn.'

In August, we said, 'It'll come in September.' We went out eagerly on exercises arranged by Group, simulating raids so bad that we drove miles to supposedly devastated areas; we sweated when we muddled up the parking arrangements, and argued frenziedly about topography.

In September, when the anniversary of those first raids was safely past, we said, 'It'll be next month: you'll see.' We swotted up our gas; we nerved ourselves to study anti-personnel bombs; we went down in parties to look at the tactical table, arranged by borough officials, to learn an entirely new method of controlling multiple incidents; we pushed toy cars about and discussed the duties and responsibilities of the all-powerful incident officer.

'Say,' said Robin, 'what happens to the party if the poor chap gets bombed?'

'Bah,' said the old hands, 'all these regulations; they'll never work. Wait till Hitler gets going in October – you'll see.'

In October, we were measured for our new uniforms; dour and unimpressed by the fact that at last we were going to get big coats and slacks and jackets, with crowns on the breast pocket, and CD for Civil Defence. What worried us was the prospect of giving clothes coupons for them. Still, we said, 'What's it matter? When the trouble comes in November, they'll be too busy to worry about coupons.'

In November, we grumbled about the coupons, about the uniforms that hadn't turned up after all, because it seemed we were all such awkward shapes we were difficult to fit, about the cold, about the cooking, about each other. We cursed because erratic hours of sleep, snatched on a stretcher, left us too weary to do the second jobs on which we counted for the extra money we needed so badly. Sometimes we said, 'There'll be raids in December, you'll see.'

'It's so awful,' Penny said, 'we can't wish we were busy because we can't be busy unless someone's hurt.'

In December, the Labour Exchanges began to draft all sorts of new people into the Service; they were called trainees;

generally they could not drive and they didn't know First Aid or Gas; they were paid the same as we were, and we had to teach them. We sighed and said the Service was changing. We grumbled about trainees, about coupons for uniforms, about the way the new coats fitted and about not even having enough of them to go round. We also grumbled about the cold and the cooking and the lack of sleep and about each other.

In December, too, a little squad of engineers suddenly began to dig like crazy terriers on the bombed site just behind us. They were looking for the unexploded bomb that had come down that Sunday night some time before. They found it, too. When they had taken its guts out, we walked over and leaned on the wooden fence and peered down into the hole, where the thing lay like a huge, shiny whale in a trap.

'There, honey,' said Robin, taking the youngest trainee firmly by the shoulders, 'take a good look. How'd you like that to land on your pet corn, baby?'

That Christmas, there was no party. Nobody felt like parties anyway, with the Germans at bay in Russia and the Japs slaughtering in the Pacific, and besides, you couldn't get cakes and crackers so easily, and no one could afford to give presents.

'Maybe it's silly to try and keep Christmas,' Robin said. And her voice was sad.

Just the same, a few of us got permission to go down to Westminster Abbey for the midnight mass. People were lining up in the square when we got there, waiting in the cold dark night as obstinately as any film queue. You had the feeling that many of them would have been too shy to go by day, so that you were aware of the strange, secret selves, hidden inside the toughest of us, charmed out at midnight by the sound of a Christmas carol.

In the Abbey there were no lights except the candles that burned on the altar; their glow brought to life the springing arches, so that you wondered if perhaps you were seeing the place as the builders intended it should look at night, all detail blurred in shadow, the pillars and buttresses dark and heavy as the weight of this world, the glow over the altar fragile and lovely as the hope of the next. People clattered about, blundering clumsily to their seats; I tripped over somebody's gas mask and lost Penny and Mark.

You did not know your neighbour; as you flashed your torch, you just glimpsed khaki and Air Force blue, the gold braid of the Navy, the shoulder badge of warden or rescue party, the crimson piping of the NFS, the flutter of a nurse's cap. And as we settled, there came the grinding of metal against stone as a thousand tin hats were stowed away.

So, in past days, generations of armed men must have come there, to cross themselves and ask a blessing or to give thanks for a safe return. Men back from the Crusades, from Agincourt, from the Armada, from Trafalgar and Waterloo, from Passchendaele and Vimy Ridge, their prayers seemed to linger there still, mingling with ours, their vivid simple faith vitalising our anaemic half-belief, as though they, the so-called dead, were far more effective than we, dulled by material cares, shackled to the machinery of modern war.

We kept quite still, as the Cross went up to the altar, just rimmed with light as it left the shadows round us. It was so dark, and we such strangers that it didn't matter if our feelings got the better of us, and if we wept as we prayed, there was no one to see.

We began to sing, 'Once in Royal David's city …' and there were tears in our voices. Once we'd been happy children, singing out the simple beliefs of our hearts. Now we were weary exiles, with years of semi-scientific thinking and modern magic and cheap philosophy and economic slogans arid about us, caught up in each other's sorrows, pricked with anxiety and numbed with suffering. As we sang, we were homesick, but homesick, for all the simple things, honour and truth and love and peace of heart.

And if we weren't very good, and hadn't much use for churches, and if our knees were stiff and our responses uncertain, and if we didn't know what we believed and what we didn't, perhaps none of that mattered, and the God so many of us still hoped to find looked kindly down on us because we brought there a great love for one another and a great homesickness for the good and simple things.

When we went away, we could not speak to one another, or make our lips say, 'Happy Christmas.'

But later on that morning, Penny and Mark and Robin and I went out into the yard of Station X2 to look for dawn. We had so often watched like this, waiting for the sunrise to pale the flames of many fires, to silence the sound of planes, to bring us quietness at last. The day came quietly, and as the shadows thinned, Penny said:

'It's Christmas; fancy keeping another Christmas in this grimy old garage.'

'Last Christmas,' Mark said, 'we thought it'd soon be over. Well, we've seen some bad nights since then. Can you believe that they really happened – to us?'

'Were you ever afraid of being bumped off?' I said.

Penny and Mark and Robin looked at each other.

'That's queer,' Mark said. 'I never was. Paralytically frightened, of course – of being *hurt*.'

'Or being sick …'

'Or falling down on the job …'

'There was a bit of me,' Penny said, 'that just didn't believe it could die, whatever happened to the rest of me. And when I was very, very frightened, that bit of me took charge.'

We knew what she meant; we had all of us been frightened enough to know what she meant. Robin lit a cigarette.

'Oh well,' she said, 'being scared and dirty and uncomfortable and tired and working together like a lot of toughs, it hasn't harmed us any.'

'I suppose,' said Mark, 'it's made us real. It hurts.'

Robin said, 'It's a funny thing, but I guess that's so. I guess earning good money and getting on and having swell friends and a good time – that sort of stuff don't seem real any more. But having good pals does. And sticking by each other and having a job of work you mind about more than you mind about yourself.'

Mark said, 'Yes, we've come to feel that way in the blitz.'

'If only,' Penny said anxiously, 'we can remember …'

'We will,' I said. The sound of my own voice surprised me but I couldn't stop. 'We will; there are so many of us, all in this together, all feeling the same way. Mark's right; we've grown real. We – we know the things that matter now, I think. Kindness and courage and loveliness, and that queer feeling of belonging to each other, minding about each other. I'm pretty sure those are the everlasting things.'

'Some of us,' said Mark slowly, 'have lost just about everything we ever cared for … even the people who were our whole life …'

'Isn't there something, somewhere,' Robin said unexpectedly, 'about having to lose your life to find it?'

'I only know,' said Penny, ' that life's never been so altogether beastly – and I've never been so happy.'

'Me too …'

Some of the men staggered out into the yard, yawning and stretching and stamping cold feet.

'Tea up, there,' they shouted. 'Tea up, girls. Tea up.'

London, 1940–1942

Notes on the text

BY KATE MACDONALD

Acknowledgment

ARP: Air Raid Precautions services, renamed Civil Defence from 1941.

I October, 1940

Five days: Before the war, post office deliveries were normally so regular and efficient that a letter posted in London in the morning would reach a south-east England destination in the afternoon.

WAAF or WRNS and ATS: the women's branches of the British air force, navy and army: the Women's Auxiliary Air Force, Women's Royal Naval Service and the Auxiliary Territorial Service.

pillar: pillar-box, the post box.

marocain: a rich stiff fabric used for evening dresses.

tweeds: a coat (jacket) and skirt made of this very warm woven wool fabric.

woollen pants: long underwear for warmth.

slacks: semi-casual women's trousers, since before the war women would only wear trousers for outdoor leisure or labouring, never for formal occasions.

mustard gas: the horrific burns and deaths caused by gas in the First World War led to a general expectation that gas would be used by Hitler's forces on civilian populations.

II October-November, 1940

blast wall: an extra wall built to minimise the impact of a direct hit.

pit-props: sturdy struts of wood to shore up ceilings and provide extra structural stability.

barrage balloons: giant silver-coloured inflatable air balloons moored to the ground, to clog up the air space above urban areas to deter bombers and other enemy planes from approaching.

Park guns: anti-aircraft gun battery located in Hyde Park near Paddington, where Ann Stafford's ambulance station was located.

Heath: Hampstead Heath, the site of the next anti-aircraft battery to the north of Paddington. It was also higher in altitude, allowing the sound of guns to reverberate across central London.

The Lambeth Walk: song from the 1937 musical comedy *Me And My Girl*, with exaggerated dance steps.

double de-clutch: a method of changing gears into neutral and then into gear, used in older and heavier vehicles with unsynchronized manual gear transmission. If Mildred had only driven cars before it would have felt very cumbersome.

pink wrapper: a pink dressing-gown.

frayed medal ribbons: showing that he fought in the First World War.

jumper pattern: *Vogue* advertised its own dress and knitting patterns for its readers to consider and then order.

reefer jacket: a short double-breasted wool overcoat.

III November 1940

Pioneers: the Royal Pioneer Corps, a unit of the British Army specialising in light engineering.

coster carts: fruit and vegetables were routinely sold in London's streets by costermongers using horse-drawn wooden carts.

crank it: to get the engine going again using the old-fashioned hand-crank.

HEs: High Explosive bombs.

Penny: her married name is Pennant. It was customary for women in professions that used formal hierarchies to call each other by their surnames, especially when they didn't know each other very well. Diminutives of surnames came about, as Mildred experiences, when professional intimacy had been achieved. But using first names was rare unless the women had known each other for many years or were related, as Mildred and Daphne were.

shingle: a short haircut for women, introduced nearly twenty years earlier when Mildred had been in her twenties.

fatigues: army term for household-related chores and general maintenance tasks, organised by rota.

char: a cleaning woman, paid by the hour to do the cleaning work.

Fords: the Ford car had been a standard inexpensive family car for decades.

incendiaries: small explosive devices dropped in large numbers from bombers, that would explode after reaching the ground, setting fire to anything flammable.

stirrup pumps: a hand-powered pump for spraying water at a fire.

siren suit: a one-piece jumpsuit or overall popularised by Winston Churchill as being convenient, warm and practical for wearing when sleeping in the bomb shelter.

mannequin: a runway model in a dress shop or fashion house.

our old felts: in a period when women over the age of 25 normally wore a hat in public, a felted wool hat was the standby: cheap, warm, tolerant of rain, in a dull colour guaranteed to go with any outfit, and unexceptional.

the rats: what Robin calls those Londoners who have abandoned the city to live in more safety in the countryside.

beetroot: the mother would have been covered in blood, but the only damp red object that the child would have encountered before would have been beetroot.

the Middlesex: the Middlesex Hospital, now demolished but was located north of Oxford Street west of Tottenham Court Road.

bread-basket: a droppable bomb dispenser that carried a load of incendiary bombs.

IV December, 1940

chilblained hands: chilblains are sores on the skin caused by extremes of heat and cold.

putting up the blackout: at dusk thick black curtains or blinds had to cover all windows and doorways where light could escape.

a break of 850: this is an improbably high score in billiards. In 1927 the then world champion Walter Lindrum scored 816 points in an unfinished break over 23 minutes, a world speed record.

speedometer reading: now called the odometer reading, recording the mileage at the start of the journey.

raspberry: military slang for a reprimand.

AFS cars: Auxiliary Fire Service cars.

OC cars: military terminology, Office Commanding, in this case, the person in charge of all vehicles.

V December, 1940

eugenists: people who believed the racist and anti-semitic theory that humans could be improved genetically by killing off those individuals with traits considered less desirable.

topography: this may be a joke about Daphne's vague grasp of the difference between geography (roads, buildings, bridges) and topography (hills, plains, rivers).

pressure point: the point on which to press to prevent blood loss from a wound.

loading: loading casualties onto and off the ambulance.

Dollis Hill: an area of north-west London.

BBC: not the British Broadcasting Corporation but probably an acronym for a mustard gas remedy.

Lewisite: a compound of arsenic manufactured as a corrosive gas that causes blisters on human tissues, against which an injectable treatment was created by British scientists in July 1940.

Fowler position: when the patient is seated on a semi-reclined position, so that the damaged abdominal area is supported well.

an area: the open basement space at the front of a terraced building, leading to a doorway into the basement floor.

Borough: the principal civil division for English towns. London has 32 boroughs.

LCC: London County Council, the umbrella local authority for London, overseeing the Boroughs.

her tib and fib: her tibia and fibula, the two long bones in the shin.

VI Christmas, 1940

forage caps: soft semi-undress uniform caps.

the ASO's maid: the ASO is from a well-off background who employs a maid; the cakes are probably a personal gift from her to the party.

VII January, 1941

Everyman's Stores: Ann Stafford's earlier novel *Business as Usual*, co-written with Jane Oliver, was set in an invented London department store called Everyman's which had strong similarities to Selfridges.

VIII January, 1941

blue-book: an official book of information on a given subject, in this case social welfare and council services.

pixie suits: all-in-one romper suits for children with distinctive pointed hoods.

show cards and fashions: she was a fashion illustrator, working for couture houses.

E M Dell: Ethel M Dell, one of the most successful and prolific British authors of the twentieth century, specialising in light and melodramatic romance.

The Good Earth: best-selling novel by Pearl S Buck about early twentieth-century rural China. The film version came out in 1937.

Damon Runyon: American journalist and short story writer who used a distinctively stylised slang and characterisation in his stories of New York street life in the first half of the twentieth century.

Nat Gould: English writer from the later Victorian period and early years of the twentieth century who became successful for his plain but masterfully told stories about Australia and horse-racing.

Obbs' *Leviathan*: Thomas Hobbes's work of political philosophy from the mid-seventeenth century.

IX February, 1941

threepennorth: three pennies-worth.

set to partners: term from country dancing, in which a couple from two lines of dancers approach and dance to each other.

potato clamps: stacks of potatoes stored in a mound, covered in straw and then soil for insulation and protection from animals.

Savoy: the Savoy Hotel offered a much classier and warmer lunch than that offered by the canteen van.

drilling: performing military marching exercises as part of their training.

two bob: two shillings, ie twenty-four pence.

square-bashing: doing endless drills and not yet being able to use that training in active service.

get their wings: the young airmen will pass their final tests and qualify as Air Force pilots, receiving the coveted wing badge for their uniform tunic.

X March, 1941

cafard: apathy or ennui.

scamp: to skimp or slack off, to not do the chores properly.

Third Line Rest Centres: places for temporarily displaced people to go after an attack or other destructive event, well away from the location of that event, while the authorities assess what they can do to find more permanent accommodation.

view hallo: the call given by the huntsman on seeing the fox ahead.

ratting: terriers were traditionally used in rat-catching. Their small bodies would make it easier for them to chase the rats into their tunnels and kill them.

XI March, 1941

drays: large carts drawn by drayhorses.

launch: small motor vessel used to transport a few people at a time, often used for pleasure cruising.

waste: cotton waste cloth, for wiping up oily messes.

rather a dab: a dab hand, skilled at.

Broads: the Norfolk Broads, which has long stretches of inland waterways.

Clacton-Margate: a popular pleasure steamer route between two seaside towns of about 30 nautical miles north to south, across the Thames Estuary.

Nore: a large sandbank just west of the point where the North Sea enters the Thames. Teddington is at the point where the Thames stops being tidal.

rankers: ordinary nurses without rank.

Thomas's splints: invented by a Welsh orthopaedic surgeon in the nineteenth century to immobilise limb fractures.

dug-out: a term from First World War trench warfare meaning a reinforced ground shelter.

XII March, 1941

queueing up: food rationing had begun in Britain in January 1940, and long queues at food shops became normal.

breaker: does she routinely drop the china while she's washing or drying it?

bant: in 1864 William Banting advocated the avoidance of fats, starch and sugar to lose wight, and banting became a term for dieting.

XIII April, 1941

mufti: civilian dress, out of uniform.

twenty-ones: Penny and Mildred are mistakenly in the queue for people who have newly turned twenty-one and are now able to register with the Labour Exchange.

we mess: military term for eating with or at.

pumps: the fire engines that pump water.

rabbit: affectionate term for a brand-new recruit.

GPO: General Post Office, who ran the telephone system and managed its switchboards.

XIV April, 1941

barrow loads: as well as fruit and vegetables flowers were sold in the streets from barrows.

settlement: a house and Christian mission staffed by volunteers and paid church workers to alleviate poverty and social deprivation in poor areas in the East End of London.

tramps: tramp steamers, freelance cargo ships that would take anything anywhere, without a regular route or clients.

W W Jacobs: English short story writer, still alive at the time *Army Without Banners* was published, who wrote about East End life and marine adventure.

Business As Usual

by Jane Oliver & Ann Stafford

Business As Usual is a delightful illustrated novel in letters from 1933. It tells the story of Hilary Fane, a newly engaged and also newly unemployed Edinburgh girl who is determined to support herself by her own earnings in London for a year, despite the resentment of her surgeon fiancé. After a nervous beginning looking for a job while her savings shrink, she finds work as a typist in the London department store of Everyman's (a very thin disguise for Selfridges). She rises rapidly through the ranks to work in the library, where she has to enforce modernising systems on her entrenched and frosty colleagues.

Business As Usual is charming, intelligent, heart-warming, funny, and entertaining. It's also deeply interesting as a record of the history of shopping in the 1930s, and for its clear-eyed descriptions of social conditions, poverty and illegitimacy.

Jane Oliver was the pen-name of Helen Rees (née Evans, 1903–1970). After working as a PE teacher and as Clemence Dane's secretary and learning to fly, Helen became a successful historical novelist. She was the widow of John Llewelyn Rhys, in whose name she founded the John Llewelyn Rhys prize for Commonwealth writers from her own royalties. (Handheld also publishes his complete works.) Ann Stafford (the pen-name of Anne Pedler, 1900–1966) also became a successful novelist. Together they published at least 97 novels.

Blitz Writing: Night Shift & It Was Different At The Time

by Inez Holden

Emerging out of the 1940–1941 London Blitz, the drama of these two short works, a novel and a memoir, comes from the courage and endurance of ordinary people met in the factories, streets and lodging houses of a city under bombardment.

Inez Holden's novella *Night Shift* follows a largely working-class cast of characters for five night shifts in a factory that produces camera parts for war planes.

It Was Different At The Time is Holden's account of wartime life from April 1938 to August 1941, drawn from her own diary. This was intended to be a joint project written with her friend George Orwell (he was in the end too busy to contribute), and includes disguised appearances by notable literary figures of the period.

The experiences recorded in *It Was Different At The Time* overlap in period and subject with *Night Shift*, setting up a vibrant dialogue between the two texts.

Inez Holden (1903–1974) was a British writer and literary figure whose social and professional connections embraced most of London's literary and artistic life. She modelled for Augustus John, worked alongside Evelyn Waugh, and had close relationships with George Orwell, Stevie Smith, H G Wells, Cyril Connolly, and Anthony Powell.

The introduction and notes are by Kristin Bluemel, Professor of English at Monmouth University, New Jersey.

There's No Story There: Wartime Writing, 1944–1945

by Inez Holden

'*There's No Story There* opens a window onto the drudgery, demands and danger of life in a massive munitions factory, some seven miles long, dubbed Statevale, located in the north of England. Both detail and mood were drawn from Holden's own experience in factory work, and her characters represent the diversity of the war machine's workforce: skilled workers, young women, men who could not enlist or have been invalided out of the army, and refugees.' — *Times Literary Supplement*

The workers make shells and bombs, and no chances can be taken with so much high explosive around. Trolleys are pushed slowly, workers wear rubber-soled soft shoes, and put protective cream on their faces. Any kind of metal, moving fast, can cause a spark, and that would be fatal.

With so much death just waiting to happen, why aren't the workers' stories told?

A companion to *Blitz Writing* (2019), Handheld Press's edition of Inez Holden's novella *Night Shift* (1941) and her wartime diaries *It Was Different At The Time* (1943), this edition of *There's No Story There* includes three pieces of Holden's long-form journalism, detailing wartime life.

'The fiction she produced in the early Forties, though framed in the decade's sharp, utilitarian light, set in factories, at town hall tribunals, in troop trains lumbering through the English countryside, often transcended their origins and veered off into an imaginative space that most of the Forties realists never penetrated ... the three short pieces included in *There's No Story There* ... are full of painstaking reportage.' — D J Taylor, *New Statesman*

Where Stands A Wingèd Sentry

by Margaret Kennedy

'This is a journal of the tense months between Dunkirk and the start of the Blitz – months when a German invasion of Britain seemed both imminent and inevitable. It's written with a steady intensity; raw worry pokes through the elegant prose, and though there are many vivid details, and moments of wit and levity, this is also an extraordinary meditation of what it means to be free in a world of encroaching tyranny.' — Lissa Evans, author of *Old Baggage, V for Victory*

Margaret Kennedy's riveting 1941 wartime memoir is *Mrs Miniver* with the gloves off. Her account, taken from her war diaries, conveys the tension, frustration and bewilderment of the progression of the war, and the terror of knowing that the worst is to come, but not yet knowing what the worst will be.

English bravery, confusion, stubbornness and dark humour colour her experiences, in which she and her children move from Surrey to Cornwall, to sit out the war amidst a quietly efficient Home Guard and the most scandalous rumours. *Where Stands A Wingèd Sentry* (the title comes from a hymn) was only published in the USA, and has never been published in the UK before.

Margaret Kennedy (1896–1967) made her name as a novelist with *The Ladies of Lyndon* (1923) and *The Constant Nymph* (1924), and continued publishing until the year before her death.